Healer

and

Witch

NANCY WERLIN

CANDLEWICK PRESS

Plant illustrations and ornaments by Joris Hoefnagel
and Georg Bocskay, sixteenth century; digital images
courtesy of the Getty's Open Content Program

First edition 2022

Library of Congress Catalog Card Number 2021946634
ISBN 978-1-5362-1956-2

21 22 23 24 25 26 LBM 10 9 8 7 6 5 4 3 2 1

Printed in Melrose Park, IL, USA

This book was typeset in Stempel Schneidler.

Candlewick Press
99 Dover Street
Somerville, Massachusetts 02144

www.candlewick.com

MIX
From responsible
sources
FSC® C103098
FSC
www.fsc.org

For Jim,
always

France

1531

CHAPTER

One

On a warm April morning, a week after the terrible day on which Grand-mère Sylvie died, Sylvie walked away from her home. She left her mother, the cottage in which they'd all lived, Bresnois village, and everyone and everything she knew. The wet spring grasses, ankle high, seemed to clutch at the hem of her skirts as if to keep her from leaving. But Sylvie kept moving. She did not look back and she did not cry. She did not deserve tears.

She had made a terrible mistake.

She'd meant no harm. Quite the reverse—she'd been trying to help her mother, Jeanne, the healer who had never before needed healing. Grand-mère Sylvie had died, and Jeanne had spent five frightening days in her chair by the fire, holding her own elbows, staring into the flames. Not eating. Not speaking.

Not crying for her mother, even when Sylvie did.

Yes, Sylvie had been trying to heal Jeanne, in her own way.

Only Sylvie's way wasn't Jeanne's way, and—she now knew—that was the problem, or one of them. Not one of the villagers would call Jeanne *witch*, not even quietly behind their hands. Jeanne as a healer and midwife possessed no mysterious powers or magic, only knowledge and caring and her deep Catholic faith.

As she walked, Sylvie pressed her fingers to her temples as if that could erase what she had done. Why had she not been more cautious? Grand-mère Sylvie had even warned her, barely three weeks before her sudden death. The memory *burned*.

Sylvie, just past her fifteenth birthday, had come finally into womanhood with her first monthly bleeding, and then the understanding—the power—

had simply appeared inside her. When she touched people, she could reach and see their thoughts and their memories. To explain, she'd held Grand-mère Sylvie's hand.

"I see you in a strange place." Grand-mère Sylvie had gone still as Sylvie added, frowning, "There are high walls—wait—are you in a kind of *prison*?"

Unhurriedly, Grand-mère Sylvie had moved her hand away, breaking the connection before Sylvie could add that she saw someone—a friend?—with her. "Never search my mind in future without my permission, my dear one."

"Of course, I shall not," said Sylvie, abashed. "I only wanted to show you. But there is more."

"I am listening."

"I think I can *remove* what I see. Grand-mère, only think! As a healer, if I can see that someone is in . . . emotional pain, about a memory? Why, I could simply take that pain away! Like—like cutting out a rotten bit of apple!" The words came out of Sylvie in an excited rush. "Is this something that you can do too—could do, I mean? Before . . ."

"Before I became old," said Grand-mère Sylvie dryly.

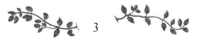

"Yes. When you laid your hands on someone in the village."

Grand-mère Sylvie shook her head. "No."

"Oh. Then—then what . . . how shall I . . ." Sylvie had not known how to formulate her next question. How was she to proceed with this new skill? She looked down trustfully into her grandmother's face, however, believing she would be understood. And she was, though Grand-mère Sylvie was quiet for a time.

"I understand your excitement, my dear one," she said at last. "Yet I counsel caution, for I believe you will need skilled guidance. I have not heard of a power like this, but I will help you sort it out, once I am a little stronger. This new gift is from God— never doubt it, or that you will use it in holiness, to heal, as the women of our family do. My own gift grew over the course of the first year or two, and as I practiced. That may be how it is with you. You are not yet fully who you will become."

Another thoughtful pause. "But, my dear one, great care will be necessary. This idea of yours about cutting out a memory so that it does not exist . . . I am not sure. Healing is complicated. Consider that

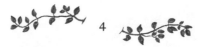

scar tissue protects a healing wound, and even after the healing, any remaining scar speaks of survival. Such scars have beauty, do they not? The reminder of what came before is often a treasure . . . but I see you do not understand. Then just remember this: to have patience, Sylvie. There are many important questions to consider before you act." Grand-mère Sylvie paused, tired merely from speaking.

"I don't think I do understand," Sylvie said, disappointed.

"You will, one day. This I know, for I know you, my dear one." Despite illness, her grandmother's voice still held all the strength that had once been in her healer's hands. She coughed before adding: "Also. There are those who will not believe your gift is from God. That will be a danger all your life, as it is for me—and for your mother by association. This you know."

"But there is no danger here in Bresnois," said Sylvie with a smile. She had heard this sort of talk before, but it seemed distant and historical.

Grand-mère Sylvie said slowly, "True, here you are much loved, like your mother. And yet caution is always warranted. And should you venture out

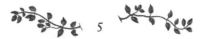

into the world, you must be careful, especially of churchmen."

Sylvie nodded; this, too, she had heard before, in stories from Grand-mère Sylvie about her life before Bresnois. But those stories seemed equally distant. As for venturing into the world, that was easily dismissed. She loved her home. But she said only, reassuringly: "Father Guillaume is our friend."

Grand-mère Sylvie sighed before nodding. "True. We are fortunate in Father Guillaume, here in Bresnois."

"And of course, I must tell my mother," said Sylvie.

"Indeed. But only when I have recovered from this illness. I need strength enough for a long talk with you both. There will be a great deal to discuss."

Sylvie nodded. "Of course."

But there had been no recovery, and no long talk.

And somehow Sylvie had not really understood she might do *harm* with her gift. Grand-mère Sylvie had spoken of scars—who would not want a scar removed?

No, she had not understood.

 6

As she walked away from her life, Sylvie made a vow to herself. She would find a teacher, an adviser, a healer. Someone who could help her with her gift as Grand-mère Sylvie no longer could.

Then she would return home. Once she understood her gift and had learned to use it properly, safely, she could restore Jeanne, so that Jeanne would regain the memories that Sylvie had taken right out of her head. The memory of Jeanne's own mother.

And also—that she had ever even had a daughter.

Two

Sylvie had not gone a mile when she heard someone calling after her. "Sylvie! Wait for me!" The voice was high, piping, and she turned, knowing whom she would see. Martin, the farrier's son, often followed her when she went to collect the wild plants that healing required. There were some things even Grand-mère Sylvie's green fingers couldn't make grow in a garden.

Even today, it lifted her heart to see Martin running after her as rapidly as his short legs would carry him.

"It's too nice to work today," Martin explained

cheerfully as he caught up. Sylvie contained a smile. Martin was incorrigibly lazy, said his father, and would never make a farrier. Though Martin liked horses and they him, he was bad at shoeing them. He would not force them because, he said, he didn't like being told what to do himself. Or even wearing shoes. And when the farrier yelled and reached for his switch, Martin would laugh and run.

Martin's eyes fastened inquisitively on Sylvie's pack and walking stick and the large pocket she wore tied around her waist—bulging slightly with cheese and bread. "Where are you going today? Can I come? I have some food. I'll share." He reached into his pocket and held out a heel of bread in one small, grubby hand.

"No, Martin," said Sylvie, wishing it were otherwise. "You can't come today."

"I have some cheese, too," wheedled Martin. He fished in the pocket again and came up with a moldy lump. "I meant it for later, but you can have it now if you really want."

"No, thank you," said Sylvie. She thought. It wouldn't hurt to have company for a few miles. "All right, come on, then." Besides, Martin had the

persistence of a puppy and always found a way to do exactly as he wished.

"Good," said Martin. He put the cheese and bread carefully away, unable to hide his relief at retaining them. The farrier did not believe in over-feeding his youngest, most worthless child. He fell into step beside her. "You looking for plants and stuff? I'll help. Maybe we'll find figs!"

"It's far too early for them," said Sylvie. And then, as Martin's face fell, she added: "But you never know."

He hummed as he walked, taking an extra hop now and then to keep up. She would send Martin back well before sunset, Sylvie thought. He would not find it odd that she stayed behind; she had slept out on fine nights before, when she really was hunting for grasses, plants, and herbs.

It was a pleasant day for walking. The way was familiar and would be for a day or more yet. They paused near noon and ate, Sylvie frugally. Martin wolfed down his own lunch and eyed the remainder of Sylvie's loaf wistfully. But she knew she would need it herself before she reached the town of Montigny.

"Why do you have so much food?" asked Martin finally, as Sylvie put the bread away.

"I'm going to be traveling a few days. Perhaps longer."

"Why? It's still cold at night."

Sylvie looked away from Martin's too-curious eyes. "Because I need to. And I'll be fine." She got up abruptly. "You must head home now, Martin. It'll take you most of the afternoon to get back to Bresnois."

Martin didn't answer. But when Sylvie began walking, he came with her. And before she could tell him again to turn back, he said, "You must miss her, yes? Your grandmother?"

After a moment, Sylvie nodded miserably. "Yes."

"Me too," Martin said simply. He kicked a stone before him, his face averted. "I used to go see her sometimes," he said. "Before she got sick. She told me once it was all right that I don't like making shoes for horses. She said . . ." His eyes flickered uneasily to left and right.

"What did she say?" asked Sylvie.

Martin mumbled, as if he were afraid of being mocked: "That she thought I wasn't meant anyway

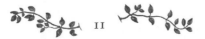

to be a farrier. That I would do something else with my life." He added, almost inaudibly: "Something special."

He was only eight, perhaps. Or nine. "Then you will," said Sylvie kindly. But Martin kicked the stone again and didn't look at her.

Several times that afternoon, as the sun began to arc away to the west, Sylvie tried to get Martin to turn back. On her fifth attempt, he stopped in his tracks, his lower lip thrusting out and his eyes dark with resentment. She felt those eyes on her as she walked away. She felt them for a long time.

It was lonely without his tuneless humming to distract her from her thoughts. Finally, as the sun dropped over the horizon, she reached the edge of the pond she'd had in mind as a campsite. It was beginning to get cold, as Martin had warned, so Sylvie carefully kindled a small fire, heated water for tea, and wrapped herself up well in Grand-mère Sylvie's big shawl. It still smelled of Grand-mère Sylvie: rosewater and lavender overlaying an almost imperceptible musk of old age. Sylvie inhaled it and closed her eyes.

She thought of Jeanne, chattering at her this

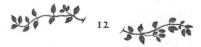

morning as if Sylvie were a chance-met acquaintance, another healer simply passing through who had needed a bed for a night. She tried not to think of the cheerful indifference with which Jeanne had handled Grand-mère Sylvie's things, including this very shawl that Jeanne herself had knitted the previous winter. "Would you like this, mademoiselle? Someone left it here, and I already have a shawl of my own." Jeanne had held the garment out to Sylvie with her characteristic generosity. "It will keep you warm."

Jeanne's personality at least was intact, Sylvie thought miserably. She had not ruined that.

Determinedly, Sylvie turned her mind to the next day and the day after, to what she must do and where she must go. She was not sure. Where might she find a healer like herself, a teacher? In Montigny? Or would she have to travel even farther from her beloved Bresnois? And how? She was mindful now of her grandmother's warnings; she could not simply ask people for what she needed. She tried to imagine what advice Grand-mère Sylvie might have given her. To avoid churchmen . . . unless, Sylvie thought rather desperately, she might

find one such as Father Guillaume. "He is one who notices the good wheresoever he looks," Grand-mère Sylvie had said of him once.

In the dusk, a toad croaked out from his lily pad across the pond and then splashed into the water. The wind whispered gently and then more force-fully, stirring the grasses and the just-budding tree limbs.

Grand-mère Sylvie might also have told her to go step-by-step. Prayer might help, too. That was what Jeanne would recommend, and Father Guillaume. Sylvie pulled the warm shawl closer around her shoulders. She wasn't sure that she *deserved* to be heard in prayer. She had never felt that before. She huddled tighter. Her action had taken part of herself away from herself.

Who was she now?

"I am a healer," Grand-mère Sylvie had said firmly when Sylvie, then eight, had asked her about the words *magic*, *sorcery*, and *witch*. "I believe God tells us what he wants of us by the gifts he gives us. It is up to us to use them for good. That is how we honor God. That is how all humans honor God."

Sylvie had meant no harm, but she had done

harm. Still, she might pray to God. Mightn't she? Pray for guidance. For help. Pray to do better with her gift.

A twig snapped sharply.

She stretched her eyes wide in the fading light and sat still, listening with all her senses, as Grandmère Sylvie and Jeanne both had taught her. She sat like that for a long time.

And finally, she heard a slight rustling that was not caused by the breeze.

It was dark now, but there was a moon and her fire, and besides Sylvie had excellent night vision. She stared at the tree twenty feet to the left, measuring the blackness of its trunk. Carefully, she examined the shadow half-hidden behind it. She sighed.

"Come out, Martin," she said.

And he did.

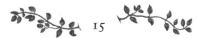

CHAPTER

Three

There was no sense being angry. It was just like Martin not to do as he was told. And he had no way of knowing that she wasn't going home soon.

But Sylvie *was* angry.

"Can I have some bread?" said Martin plaintively, and she snarled at him.

"It's more than you deserve! How dare you follow me?"

Martin had crouched down by the fire on his bare heels. He looked right back at her, his shoulders taut, hunched, protective. "I felt like it."

Sylvie's fists clenched. She unworked them, sat down again by her fire, and took a deep breath. She got out the bread, impatiently pulled off a hunk, and threw it in his general direction as hard as she could. He caught it neatly, tore into it, and didn't say thank you.

"You go back in the morning," Sylvie said. "Do you understand me?"

Martin made a motion with his hands to indicate that he was chewing and couldn't speak. It infuriated her all over again. She pulled off some bread and ate it herself. She watched him narrowly. He was eating too fast; he'd be done in no time and want more, no doubt. Well, he couldn't have any more. Thoughtless, disrespectful, disobedient . . . *child*.

And now look. He was starting to shiver. He hunched himself into a tight ball, thin arms around knobby knees beneath thin cloth, teeth working hard on the last bits of crust. His eyes skimmed Sylvie's face and rested a single wistful moment on the remainder of the bread.

No wonder the farrier beat him. Sylvie pushed over the remainder of the loaf, flung her grandmother's warm shawl in Martin's direction, and went to hunt more twigs for the fire.

17

Just after sunrise, Martin redeemed himself by catching a large fish. He had it cleaned and cooking on a rock in the rekindled fire before Sylvie, who'd slept poorly, was completely awake. It smelled wonderful and tasted that way too. They ate it all.

"I can catch another anytime," Martin boasted. "I just wade into the shallows and put my hands down and wait, and then, when one comes along . . ." He mimed grabbing a fish and throwing it onto the bank. "You have to be fast. I'm always fast." He paused, and then added almost apologetically: "Sometimes you have to wait a long time before one comes along, though."

"It's a good trick," Sylvie said grudgingly. "Useful."

"I can teach you, Sylvie," said Martin eagerly. "It's not so hard."

Sylvie shook her head. "No, I have to be getting on. And it'll take you all day to get back to Bresnois."

Martin was silent. He poked at the dying fire with a stick, reigniting it momentarily.

"Martin," said Sylvie. But he wouldn't look at her.

Sylvie sighed. She got sand and put out the fire. She picked up Grand-mère Sylvie's shawl from where she and Martin had slept, sharing its warmth, and folded it carefully.

Martin watched until Sylvie was done, until she turned, finally, and looked straight at him. "It's time for you to go, Martin. I mean it."

For another long moment she thought he would stay there, like yesterday, until she was forced to turn her back and walk away from him. But then he got up too. And said quietly, seriously: "You're running away, Sylvie. Aren't you."

Not a question. He knew. Sylvie flushed. "Not *running*. Just . . . just going. For a while. I have to."

He said, "But doesn't your mother need you?"

Not anymore, Sylvie thought. "I don't think she does," she said. "And I have something else important that I must do." She cleared her throat. "So. Now you know. I won't be going back. Well, I *will*, but not for a long time."

Martin nodded. He was so serious he almost didn't seem like himself. "When I saw you leaving yesterday," he said, "I knew. I knew you were going."

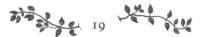

There was something slightly alarming about his calm. He did not even ask why she was going. "You can't come," said Sylvie. "You *can't*."

"Yes, I can," said Martin. And he smiled, a big, wide Martin grin. "I never wanted to be a farrier, anyway," he said. "I told you. They don't need me either. And you know what, Sylvie?"

It was hopeless. She couldn't force him to go back. She couldn't make him do anything. "What?" said Sylvie.

"I'll teach you to fish," said Martin.

It would be four days before they reached the town of Montigny, and well before then Sylvie was guiltily glad for Martin's cheerful company. He kept her from brooding. Once she taught him what to look for, he was adept at spotting the plants she always kept an eye out for, and one evening he snared a rabbit for dinner. He was so proud of himself that Sylvie hadn't the heart to tell him that she was usually too fond of rabbits to eat them.

Besides, it wasn't too bad, if you were hungry and kept your mind on other things.

Another good thing about Martin was that he

didn't ask questions. Having established that Sylvie was leaving home, leaving her mother, he left it at that. He wasn't even curious about where they were going—a good thing, since after Montigny, Sylvie herself was not sure. "I've never been any-where before," he said happily one morning, out of nowhere. He squinted ahead at the hills, purple in the distance before them. He listened rapt to Sylvie's stories about the one time she'd traveled to Montigny for midsummer fair. Jeanne had bought a donkey, and Sylvie had eaten so many sweets she was sick behind a market stall.

"It was a little like market day in Bresnois," Sylvie said. "But so big! There were things you never heard of, or even imagined. Do you know what an orange is?" Martin shook his head. "They're round and saffron-colored and about so big," said Sylvie, showing him the size with her hands. "When you cut one open, it bleeds like the juiciest meat. And when you bite into it, it's tart. Tart like . . ." She laughed. "I don't know like what. But it's sweet, too. I can't describe it."

"You ate one?" said Martin, wide-eyed.

Sylvie nodded. "We shared a whole one, just us

three. Grand-mère Sylvie had eaten them before." She paused. "And that was just the food, Martin. There was so much else to see. Strange animals. I saw one like a horse, but it had a hump on its back. And there was a little animal, like a manikin almost, very small and hairy, with feet like tiny hands." Sylvie laughed again. "And I saw—oh! Cloth merchants and jewelers and candlemakers and a weaver, and there was a fortune-teller, and even fine lords and ladies were shopping and walking and seeing the sights, just like everyone else."

They walked in silence for a while.

"Will we see a fair, do you think?" asked Martin finally. "I'd like to."

"Maybe we will." Sylvie paused, remembering an old fantasy. "Maybe if we found a fair, we could set up our own booth. I could sell remedies. I know potions for ague, for the red rash, and for choler. And some other things, too, like boils and sties. I can make eye baths. Remove splinters."

"I could walk around the fair," Martin said, "and tell people how wonderful your remedies are. I'd tell them you saved me from certain death! They'd all come running! We'd be rich!"

Sylvie laughed. "What good would being rich do us?"

Martin picked up a blade of grass and began chewing it thoughtfully. "Lots. Sylvie, if you could make love potions, then we'd really be rich. Love is what everyone wants." He smirked. "Like my sisters."

Sylvie shook her head. "Grand-mère Sylvie always said love potions were nonsense. My mother too. You cannot force someone else to care for you."

"Huh." Martin's expression said he wasn't sure whether to believe her. But then he said: "Couldn't you concoct something, anything, and just *tell* people it's a love potion?"

"No!" Sylvie was indignant. "That would be lying—false healing!"

"Just asking," said Martin, with his hands up.

But their talk did set Sylvie thinking. She had a few silver coins with her, which had belonged to Grand-mère Sylvie. She was not sure how much they would buy, or how long they might last. But now that she was responsible, also, for Martin, the small amount began to worry her. Perhaps in

Montigny they could find a way to earn more. It would not be a bad thing to earn some coins, while she tried to plan what to do next. The town was expensive; she remembered that quite well.

It was worrisome. And Martin was such a little boy. How could she have brought him with her? It had been selfish of her. And how was she to find a teacher, someone like Grand-mère Sylvie? Was there anyone else like her, like Sylvie, in all the world? Even if there was, the world was a large place.

That night before she slept, Sylvie reached out for Martin's hand. He was already asleep, muttering something indistinguishable in his dreams, his hand hot and a bit damp. She held it gently but firmly for just a moment, and then released it.

Whatever happened, she would take care of Martin.

Four

Sylvie dreamed a memory.

It was a dark night, and Sylvie was sitting beside Grand-mère Sylvie, who was ill, trying to coax her into swallowing one more spoonful of bean soup. Then, fighting the wind, someone forced the door open and then shut behind her. Jeanne, with her cheeks red and cold; she had been gone some time. She had firewood with her, and she knelt and stacked it carefully by the hearth. She stripped off her cloak and her mittens and began to warm herself silently.

"Well?" said Grand-mère Sylvie. Her voice was a mere thread, but it carried.

Jeanne turned, still on her knees. "Gervase died," she said. "I couldn't help." She shrugged, half turned away again, her face profiled in the firelight. Sylvie knew it was not indifference, that shrug. Jeanne was anything but indifferent.

"You cannot heal everybody," croaked Grand-mère Sylvie. "Every healer knows that. We learn it early." She sighed, her eyes for a moment faraway.

Jeanne said to the fire, "If you had let me take Sylvie—"

"No," said Grand-mère Sylvie sharply.

Jeanne's jaw tightened. "She is a woman now, nearly. And at her age, you took me—"

"Sylvie is not you. Right now, she should not be helping to take care of people."

Sylvie wanted to protest, but held her tongue.

Jeanne stood up abruptly. She took a deep, heavy breath. "Maman—"

"You don't understand, Jeanne," said Grand-mère Sylvie.

Jeanne snapped, "That's right, I don't! Gervase didn't say a word, do you understand that? Not one. Gervase, who complains when he stubs his toe! If I could just have gotten him to fight, if I—

26

but I couldn't. I couldn't stir him, not as you could. But Sylvie is like you; that's clear now. Perhaps she could have done something. How do we know if we don't try? Gervase has a family—"

"That is enough, Jeanne." Grand-mère Sylvie appeared unmoved. "You have to trust my judgment."

"Maman. You're old and tired. Sick. You will not be here much longer with us." She ignored Sylvie's indrawn, shocked breath, for this was the first time it had been said out loud, and to Sylvie it was a surprise. Jeanne stood tall and straight, with only a slight check in her voice betraying that this was difficult for her, too. "What about *my* judgment? You—I'm sorry—you may not be seeing things clearly."

There was silence. Sylvie watched her mother's eyes duel with her grandmother's.

"What harm," added Jeanne desperately, "could it possibly do if Sylvie tries, just tries—"

"Sylvie cannot go to people now unless I am there with her," croaked Grand-mère Sylvie.

"Then it's *me* you don't trust!" said Jeanne. "To train my own daughter—"

"No, my dear, no—"

"You've never thought I was any good as a healer!" said Jeanne. "You've always been disappointed, always wished I were more like you—"

"No!"

"Oh, I should have gone with Marc, I should have married him and taken Sylvie and gone away, I should never have stayed here and tried to be like you, for I cannot be like you, I have always disappointed you—"

"My dear, no."

"And you!" Suddenly Jeanne's gaze fixed on Sylvie, burning like ice. "I'm your mother, I gave birth to you, it was my decision, I wanted you, but *she* is the one that you talk to, share with . . . you went to *her* a few weeks ago when your woman's bleeding came. Not to me."

Sylvie bit her lip guiltily. "But then I told you." She had not told Jeanne about her gift, however.

"Second. You told me second. And now Gervase is dead," said Jeanne. "And he might not be, if you had helped me, Sylvie. If you had tried." She turned away. She hiccupped.

In the quiet Sylvie could hear the fire crackling. She got up and went to her mother, hugging her from behind. Jeanne's hand came up and grasped hers, tightly, but she would not turn. Her whole body shook.

"It's hard to lose someone," said Grand-mère Sylvie. "I understand, my dear. I understand. It's not your fault. Or Sylvie's."

Jeanne wept. Sylvie stroked her. And heard her add, so softly that only Sylvie could hear: "But why won't you try, my little one? Why do you let her stop you? It was a life at stake. I don't understand. I don't understand."

"Sylvie! Sylvie, wake up! Let go!"

In her dream, she had taken hold of Martin's hand again, so tightly she was hurting him. Sylvie took a deep, shaky breath, gathering herself. "I'm sorry," she said.

"I have bad dreams sometimes too," said Martin.

Miserably, Sylvie nodded.

Martin considered. "You can hold my hand again, if you like. Just—not so hard?"

Despite herself, Sylvie smiled. She took Martin's hand and squeezed it very gently before releasing it. "I'm all right now. Thanks for waking me."

"S'nothing." He was already drowsing.

Sylvie did not sleep now. Instead, she thought.

They would be in Montigny soon. They would need to find someplace to stay for a day or two. They would need to buy provisions. Maybe earn some coins; they were young and strong and there must be some kind of work they could do. And she must begin—carefully—to find the teacher she needed.

She reached out again and gently touched Grand-mère Sylvie's shawl, wrapped around Martin. He held the shawl against his cheek in one fist as if it were a cuddle rag. She took a corner of it in her own fist, curled up next to Martin, and closed her eyes.

When she woke, she knew how she would begin to search for the person she needed in Montigny. And if there was no one in Montigny, then she would go to a bigger town and ask there. Someone would know someone. Eventually.

She leaned over to wake Martin up.

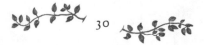

The moment they walked into Montigny, Martin's jaw dropped farther than Sylvie would have thought physically possible—and stayed there as he stared, openmouthed, at sight after sight. The town wall, with its guarded main gate, and the armed soldier stationed there whose sharp gaze cut right through them. The cobbled streets, so many that it would take an entire day to walk them all. A rattletrap inn by the town square, where a sad-eyed nag hung its head over the stable-yard fence while the land-lady's scolding voice traveled through the inn's open door: "What do you mean we're out of sausage? We've guests to feed! Run down to the butcher immediately!"

"Sausage?" said Martin, stopping dead. He eyed Sylvie hopefully. His bare toes curled against the unfamiliar stone pavement. Sylvie had shoes. Did Martin need them, now that they were in a town? Sylvie wondered. She knew he would not *want* them.

"They've run out of sausage," she said.

"They're getting more," said Martin stubbornly. He pointed. "Look." A young woman scurried out

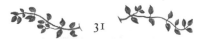

of the inn's side door, moved rapidly across the town square, and disappeared into a butcher's shop. "Maybe they'd feed us if I took care of that horse for them. Or else I could—"

"I have some coins. One will buy us sausage," said Sylvie slowly, thinking of how little they had been eating, weighing it against how few coins she had.

"And bread?"

"And bread," said Sylvie. "This one time."

The landlady frowned at them when they went in and stood awkwardly by the door, but she became cordial enough after Sylvie said they wished to buy breakfast. "With sausage," said Martin, and the landlady positively beamed at him.

"Sit down right over there," she said, indicating the unoccupied end of the inn's long, heavy table. "Good. And yes, there'll be plenty of sausage for you and your big sister, if you don't mind a bit of a wait."

"Oh, we're not—" began Sylvie. She stopped because Martin kicked her under the table.

"We don't mind waiting," he said smoothly. "My sister"—he didn't look at Sylvie, but she felt

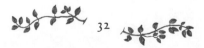

another sharp kick—"has been promising me sausage for days."

Martin was right, Sylvie realized. They didn't need to have a long discussion with the landlady about who they were, and this would avoid it. She said, "My brother thinks of nothing but food," and was rewarded by an approving smile from Martin. Mischievously, she added, "He's so tiresome," and watched with satisfaction as indignation replaced the smile on Martin's face.

"Now, now, don't fight," said the landlady. "And just help yourselves to what's there." She bustled off, and Martin reached for the bread, still glaring at Sylvie.

Sylvie grinned at Martin and handed him a mug. They couldn't talk freely; there were two or three men sitting at the table as well, drinking ale and talking business, and perhaps also waiting for sausage. She listened idly as she nibbled on her second piece of bread and Martin devoured his third.

An accountant to a rich merchant dominated the conversation. Yves, he seemed to be called. Yves the accountant was full of boasts about his master's latest venture—a large caravan that would carry

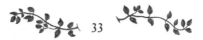

33

cloth, spices, and tapestries to Marseille by way of
Lyon. They waited only to hire two more guards
to protect the caravan against robbers as it went
through the mountains. Yves bragged that he was
to be Monsieur Chouinard's second-in-command to
the expedition, not merely an accountant, because
he had bought a share in the venture. When he was
as rich as his master, he said, he would invite them
all to a better meal at a better inn than this one.

Sylvie saw the landlady's face and winced.
Minutes later, the landlady discreetly refreshed
Yves's ale with a healthy gobbet of spit. Sylvie
looked down and hastily bit her lip. Oh, how her
mother and grandmother would laugh when Sylvie
told them—oh.

For a minute, she had to sit very still and simply
breathe.

More bread arrived, with butter, and then finally
the sausage, and with it the landlady came and
lingered with them for a minute. Sylvie squirmed
inside, appetite gone, as Martin glibly invented
answers to the landlady's questions about their
family origin and travels.

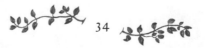

If they were going to keep this up and let people think they were brother and sister, they would need to agree on a story. Sylvie could not leave Martin in charge of it.

His presence did complicate things.

CHAPTER

Five

While Martin befriended the nag in the stable yard, Sylvie questioned the landlady.

"A healer," said the woman doubtfully. "The apothecary does most everything around here to help folks with aches and pains. Pulled my tooth out for me last year." She opened her mouth and pointed out the gap. "I was never so glad to lose anything in my life. I thought I'd die of the pain."

Sylvie hesitated—she could ask this apothecary, for surely he would know the competition—but decided to press the landlady just a bit. "I meant . . . more of a wisewoman. Or a midwife, perhaps."

The landlady's gaze sharpened. Her eyes flew to Sylvie's thin waist. "Ah," she said merely, but it was easy to read her mind and Sylvie suddenly, helplessly, blushed.

As Sylvie watched, the landlady's canny face filled with unexpected compassion. She steered Sylvie inside the kitchen. "Men!" she said to Sylvie in a low voice. "I suppose he spoke of marriage, did he not? Or was it worse than that, and you only just budding into womanhood? Fie on him, the cad!"

Sylvie opened her mouth and then closed it. Her cheeks—her whole body—burned fiercely hot.

As a daughter and granddaughter of midwives, Sylvie was not innocent about how it was that babies were made. She understood that the landlady thought that Sylvie was unhappily pregnant, as a result of seduction—or even worse, rape—and needed assistance from a wisewoman so that there would be no baby. But her blush was not because of what the landlady assumed, or not only.

It was because this was a good woman to whom Sylvie was not going to tell the truth.

"There is no need to say any more," said the landlady kindly. "Do not think that I am one to

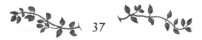

shake a finger in private. You are too young to know how to judge a good man or how to defend yourself against the bad."

I never used to be a liar, Sylvie thought. She listened numbly as the landlady told her in low, confidential tones about where Sylvie might find someone called Ceciline.

"Thank you, madame," said Sylvie finally. She could scarcely stand this. "Thank you."

But the landlady would not let go of her arm. Her brow was furrowed. She looked intensely into Sylvie's eyes. "I was young once and have not forgotten," she said.

Sylvie waited to be released.

"You had better come right back here," said the landlady at last. "After Ceciline. You and your brother both. I can find room for you for a few days. The boy can help out while you rest. I will advise you about men." She leaned in. Her grip almost hurt. "With a man, you must be the one who chooses, rather than letting yourself be chosen. My husband, you will say he does not look like much, but he knows my worth as a partner. We have built up this inn together. You must find one such as he, who

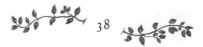

respects you. Also, it is not a bad idea for a young woman to carry a secret knife for protection."

She now seemed to be waiting for a reply.

"A secret knife," Sylvie echoed, leaving completely alone the topic of a husband. Finding a suitable one could not have been further from her thoughts or desires. But the landlady was not to know that. Many girls her age and class did marry, of course, or hoped rather desperately to do so in the future. It was the way of a normal life. But Sylvie had grown up knowing that she could choose another path, as her mother and grandmother had. She had long since decided to marry only when she was quite old, twenty-five or thirty, and then only if she had someone particular—and irresistible—in view. She almost wanted to laugh hysterically. Sylvie actually did carry a good knife in her pack of belongings, though it was for collecting her plant samples and other general uses like eating, not defense.

"Yes, a secret knife." The landlady, who was clearly a city girl, tapped her thigh significantly. "Strapped in a sheath under your skirt. And mind you keep it sharp and ready." Her eyes glinted

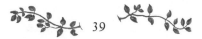

with some remembered satisfaction. Finally, she let Sylvie go. She wiped her hands on her apron, frowning again. "I'd accompany you today if I could. That Ceciline's a tricky one."

Sylvie managed to say: "Martin—my brother will be with me."

"I suppose he's better than nothing," said the landlady doubtfully. "Come straight back here afterward. Promise me!"

"You're so kind. But I—I'm not sure—"

"You must," said the landlady firmly. "You will need to rest. You will need a woman looking after you." Seeing Sylvie's reluctance, she moved, her formidable bulk blocking the door. "If you won't promise to come back, I won't let you go until I can take you there myself."

Sylvie gave in and nodded acceptance. It was warming, she told herself, to see the truth of what she had learned from Jeanne and from Grand-mère Sylvie: that in private, women helped women. That the help she was being offered was not quite the help she needed mattered not.

Then, suddenly, she wondered if Martin believed that *he* was protecting *her*, if that was a reason he

had come. Like arms imprisoning her from behind, a new feeling of vulnerability squeezed her chest, taking her breath.

She had never felt this way at home.

She did not like it.

"Thank you," Sylvie said simply to the landlady, and laid a hand on her heart. "I had to come here to the city, and yet it may have been as foolish as it was necessary. But I have been fortunate indeed to meet you, madame, and your kind heart."

"Of course, you have been foolish," said the landlady, suddenly brusque. "On several counts. But sometimes—not always—our Lord Jesus Christ protects the foolish. And at the same time, our Lord helps those who help themselves. So they say, and so I believe." She stepped back, smoothing her hands on her apron and telling Sylvie how much she should pay Ceciline. "And see that you give her not a *sol* more than that! I'll expect you for the evening meal. That young one"—she jerked her chin toward the door, toward Martin—"will be hungry." And finally, the landlady was gone to her busy day.

Sylvie took three deep, steadying breaths and went to fetch Martin.

CHAPTER
Six

Still filled with shame at having deceived the landlady, Sylvie was in no hurry to find the wise-woman Ceciline. She let Martin lead, let him explore the noisy, winding, cluttered city streets.

Martin was particularly delighted with the market. He watched for long minutes in fascination as the carpet maker deftly loomed a pile of dun-colored hemp into a neat, utilitarian square. He paused to listen to the nut seller sing the praises of his fruit. He lingered beside a particular bakery cart, nostrils twitching at the cunning twists of still-warm pastry. He followed a mule who was stolidly carting potatoes. And everywhere he went, Sylvie noticed, people smiled and winked at him and said good morning and expressed astonishment at his head of tight, bright carrot curls. Everyone seemed instantly charmed by Martin and his exuberance.

Everyone, that is, except a tall, broad-shouldered young man wearing a richly embroidered blue surcoat. The young man had reason to be displeased, Sylvie admitted to herself: Martin, distracted, had run full tilt into him. There was a moment when it seemed they would both go down in the mud.

Then the young man found his balance, grasped Martin by his grubby forearms, lifted him as if he weighed three feathers, and set him safely on his feet. Martin started to smile up at him, and maybe to apologize.

But the cool look in the rich young man's eyes froze Martin's smile. Dismissively, the young man spoke. "Heed your surroundings, boy." Fastidiously brushing off his hands as if he had touched dung instead of boy, he said something under his breath to his shorter, stouter, older, and far less well-dressed companion, whom Sylvie was startled to recognize

as Yves the accountant, swallower of the landlady's spit. Yves had exchanged his self-satisfied smirk for an obsequious one.

The haughty young man was moving on, but Martin's eyes flared. His hands fisted. Sylvie stepped forward hastily and grabbed one of them. She held it firmly.

"Martin," she said. "I suppose we could afford a pastry. Shall we get one and share it?"

Martin tore his resentful gaze from the blue surcoat as it disappeared into the market throng. He nodded stiffly. Relieved, Sylvie tugged him in the opposite direction. She would need to speak to Martin later about the importance of controlling his temper. Later would be soon enough, of course.

As Martin finished his last buttery bit of pastry, a boy selling eggs reached out and touched Martin's red hair. "It means you're good luck," he said. "Or it means you're a troublemaker. Which?"

Martin laughed, fully himself again. "Troublemaker," he caroled, dancing away backward, as heedless as before.

"Me too!" said the egg-boy. He grabbed up a precious goose egg, took a few backward steps of

his own, and held up the egg, poised. "Catch it if you can!" he called to Martin, and let fly.

Martin leaped up and snatched the egg, whole, out of the air. He held it up delicately between his fingers, the fingers that could snatch a fish live from the water.

Around them in the plaza, people burst into scattered applause and laughter. Martin bowed deeply. Then he rose—and suddenly and unexpectedly, he lobbed the egg back toward the egg-boy.

The egg-boy ducked, which wasn't necessary because the egg sailed an easy ten inches above where his head had been, to land with a smart crack on the front of a certain richly embroidered blue surcoat.

Sylvie clapped a hand to her mouth.

Everyone but the chickens and pigs stared as the thick yellow yolk of the goose egg slithered its way downward, impeded here and there by pieces of eggshell and now-ruined threads of embroidery.

Sylvie thought she saw a flicker of emotion on the young man's face—shame? Or—but it couldn't be—amusement? But she must have been mistaken, because, no, his face was a cool mask, and he did not

45

so much as look down at the egg. Instead, he sent a single long, comprehensive glance around the market, seeming to take note of every person present. Sylvie thought that he should not have been able to dominate the crowd with such a glance. Surely, he was not more than six or seven years older than she was?

Finally, his gaze settled inevitably and unerringly on Martin.

"You," said the young man.

One would have had to know Martin as well as Sylvie to interpret the tilt of his chin as anything but insolence. Sylvie braced herself, trying to think of something to do, and failing.

"Trouble," moaned the egg-boy under his breath.

Without moving his eyes from Martin's face, the man said, "Who is responsible for this small boy?" For all that it carried, his voice was level.

It was only a few steps to Martin's side. Sylvie took them. She felt the young man's gaze weigh her and find her wanting.

She raised her chin. "He's my brother," she said to the rich young man. "It was an accident." She sneaked a look at the still-dripping yolk. It had

nearly reached the man's waist. The stain would never come out.

Good.

"Indeed, he's sorry," she said. She put a pleading note in her voice, even though she hated doing it. The young man's brow lifted in mocking disbelief, while Martin said nothing.

"Very sorry," Sylvie insisted. Beneath her skirt, she trod viciously on Martin's toes. "Martin?"

Martin muttered something inaudible that might perhaps have passed for an apology, but probably not, and Sylvie spared a moment to reflect that if this horrible young man failed to murder Martin, she herself could do it later with her bare hands.

Time stretched.

At last the young man strolled forward, booted foot by booted foot. The heavy leather boots stopped in front of Martin, but their occupant looked down on both of them, though Sylvie was grown as tall as any woman. He reached into his pocket and pulled out an exquisite silk handkerchief.

He squatted in front of them with the grace of perfect physical control—Sylvie found she hated him for that, too—and held out the handkerchief

to Martin. "Wipe it up, boy," he said. There was no expression on his face at all, no clue to his thoughts, just the stillness.

Martin made no move to take the handkerchief. The delicate ivory fabric trembled in the spring breeze.

"Martin," said Sylvie, for some reason now truly feeling desperate. "Please." She snatched for the handkerchief herself, but the young man moved it unhurriedly just out of her reach.

"I'll wait," he said calmly. "The boy will do it."

Sylvie felt the hatred swell higher inside. "No, he won't," she said, and somehow the pleading tone of before had left her voice and the words came out defiant. The young man turned his head and looked at her with interest for the first time. Sylvie thought again of the secret knife she didn't have strapped to her thigh. She reminded herself that healers did not kill, even if sorely tempted.

In that instant Martin reached for the handkerchief.

Sylvie's whole stomach heaved in relief.

Martin held the handkerchief as gently as he had the egg. He lifted it level with the young man's

rich blue surcoat, at the beginning of the egg stain. He dabbed at the stain carefully, his fingers rigid. Sylvie reached for and grasped his other hand. He let her.

At last it was over. Martin held out the begrimed handkerchief.

The young man shook his head and stood up. "Keep it," he said. "And in future, watch yourself." He turned back to his companion, Yves the accountant, who was studying the ground as intently as if he could read his future there. "You had a report on the alum supplies controlled by Venice," the young man said to Yves.

"Oh yes, yes."

Sylvie put her hand on Martin's shoulder. They watched the young man walk away with his accountant.

The show was over; the market returned to normal. Sylvie said to Martin, "I know you didn't want to do that. But I'm glad you did. We don't need trouble. Not with a rich person. Do you see?" Her frustration and fear were still in her voice.

Martin had clenched his hand completely around the handkerchief, crushing it, regardless of

the wet, sticky yellow stains now on his hands. He looked up at Sylvie but didn't answer.

"Don't cry, Martin," said Sylvie urgently. "Don't cry."

Martin swallowed. "I saw him," he said. "I saw him and—and I aimed."

"I know. Why?"

"I don't know! Because I wanted to. Because I *could*. I didn't really think about what came next."

"Oh." For there was nothing she, of all people, could find to say to that.

Martin marched over to the egg-boy. He opened his hand and the ivory silk handkerchief dropped silently on top of the perfect pyramid formed by the whole speckled eggs. "I broke your egg," he said. "I can't pay, but the handkerchief is worth something. When it is clean."

"But it was my fault," said the egg-boy, making no move to pick up the dirty silk. "I threw the egg to you in the first place. I thought it would break then."

Martin shrugged. "But I was the one who broke it." He was staring at the handkerchief. Slowly, he picked it up again and put it in his pocket.

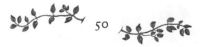

Sylvie asked the egg-boy, "Who was that man?"

The egg-boy was eager to talk. "His name is Chouinard."

Of course. This was the master Yves the accountant had bragged of at the inn. The merchant who was organizing the large caravan to carry cloth, spices, and tapestries southward. She ought to have guessed, but she had thought the sponsor of such an expedition would be, well . . . *older.* More like Yves: short, stout, and . . . well, not so impressive.

"He lives here in Montigny, this Monsieur Chouinard?" asked Sylvie. Beside her, Martin said nothing, but she knew he was listening intently.

"Sometimes. He has a big house here. But he's a nobody, who does not even know the name of his own father." Though the egg-boy's words were firm, his tone was not. He looked uneasily around. "Well. No one talks about that anymore. It's true, though. He's a bastard." Strident now, his voice. He leaned forward. "He went away. He was—I don't know—just my age, or even younger. He was nothing then. Nobody. But a handful of years later, he's *Monsieur* Chouinard. And . . ." He rubbed his fingers

together significantly. "So we bow and scrape, here in Montigny. But we do not forget."

He paused and grinned at Martin and added, low, "Perhaps not all were sad, just now, to see him egged."

"Oh," said Sylvie.

"He has other houses, too, so they say," said the egg-boy. "In Venice. And Bruges. Paris. Forty men work for his business here in Montigny. Some say . . ." He dropped his voice again.

"What?"

"Some say it's unnatural. You can't become rich out of nowhere. You should not rise above your given place in the world. So perhaps there is sorcery in it somewhere, or the work of the devil."

Sylvie's shoulders stiffened. She did *not* want to hear more on that topic. As to Monsieur Chouinard's parentage, well, Jeanne had chosen not to marry Sylvie's father. She took a step back from the gossipy egg-boy. After all, what did it matter about this man, this Chouinard? She and Martin would not see him again. They had their own concerns. Why had she even asked?

"Come, Martin," she said. "We should be going."
Stiffly, she thanked the egg-boy.

Martin followed her out of the market, his feet dragging.

It was getting late, Sylvie thought. And she, too, was tired. But it was past time to find the healer, the wisewoman Ceciline.

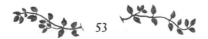

CHAPTER

Seven

By taking three steps to her two, Martin kept abreast of Sylvie as they wound their way through the dusty, narrow alleys below the western tower of Montigny's wall. It was different from the friendly market area. Here, people hurried past with their heads lowered and without a greeting for each other, let alone for strangers—even if the stranger was a small boy with red hair. Here, the lowering sun seemed to have difficulty finding its way around the tight buildings to reach the pavement, and the cheerful clatter of the market was replaced by a low sullen mutter, punctuated by an occasional sharp wail from an unseen child or the harsh voice of an angry husband. Here, according to the landlady of the inn, lived Ceciline the wisewoman.

Several times Sylvie opened her mouth to ask Martin how he was feeling, or to warn him to avoid Monsieur Chouinard—in fact, to run the other way and hide if he should see him—for the remainder of their time in Montigny. But Martin's lips were pressed together in a thin white line, and his small forehead wore a heavy frown of thought, so Sylvie said nothing. For now.

What could Martin be thinking? He was just a child, and the truth was, he had done wrong. The punishment hadn't been unfair or even cruel, Sylvie thought now. And certainly Martin had been through punishments far more painful. The farrier whipped him regularly; she knew that for a fact. It was just young Monsieur Chouinard's aspect that had been so alarming. She sighed.

"Could this be it?" asked Martin suddenly. "There's a yard. Sort of." He'd dropped a few steps behind and was pointing into an entryway that Sylvie had passed without really seeing. She went back. Martin was right. Tight and unpromising

though the entry was, it formed the mouth of a tiny courtyard. A tumbledown stone house, with windows like lidless eyes, stood on the other side. "She's got the only cobblestone yard in that part of town," the landlady had said, as resentful as if her inn didn't have a big courtyard of its own.

A peculiar stillness descended the moment they set foot in the courtyard. Sylvie twitched. She couldn't like the place. Martin, too, was dawdling. "Come on," she said to him. There were only a couple more hours of daylight. "Let's see if she's home." They crossed the courtyard, lifted the clumsy iron door knocker, and let it fall three times.

Sylvie did not expect a response. Or maybe it was that she suddenly did not want one. In her mind, she and Martin were already retracing their steps across the courtyard, into the alleys of west Montigny, and back to the safety of the inn and the welcome of its landlady. When there was no response to her third knock, she turned with relief to go.

"Good afternoon," said a low, laughing voice behind them. "I'm here. Didn't you want me after all?"

 56

Sylvie turned back and gasped. There in the open doorway of the stone house stood the most beautiful woman imaginable. She was as tall as Sylvie, her head nearly brushing the arch, and her straight graceful limbs were swathed in yards and yards of a thin black fabric. Laughter seemed to surround her. It took several seconds before Sylvie realized that, although her hair was untouched by gray, the skin of her face and hands and of her slender neck was softly crumpled with age.

This, then, was Ceciline.

But Ceciline, too, was staring. She stared for a long time. Then she spoke. "But it's Sylvie. Sylvie, young again . . ." The wisewoman lifted a hand to her own cheek. "Sylvie's daughter?" she asked. "No. Granddaughter?"

It was a miracle. "Yes," Sylvie said. "I am her granddaughter." Relief filled her. Not only was this woman a healer, she knew Grand-mère Sylvie! She said eagerly to Ceciline: "You knew her?"

Ceciline nodded. "A long time ago." She hesitated. "You said 'knew.' Sylvie is dead, then?"

"Yes," Sylvie said, and watched the woman's gaze shutter, just for a second.

Then, although she was clearly having trouble speaking, Ceciline said, "Sylvie's granddaughter is welcome here."

Sylvie said, "I also am called Sylvie. This is my friend, Martin."

Ceciline managed a smile for Martin, who was staring dumbly. Then she gestured them inside her house.

It was a single large room, well swept but rather bare, with a wooden ladder fastened to one wall and leading up to a loft. An unusually subdued Martin sat down on a stool, but Sylvie remained standing. Her gaze was drawn to the windows, beneath which struggled a very few, very common garden plants. Thyme, basil. Chamomile. She thought of Grand-mère Sylvie's extensive medicinal garden. Grand-mère Sylvie could never have lived in a town, with only an uneasy bare courtyard like Ceciline's.

As if she could read Sylvie's mind, Ceciline came up to her and said: "We were never alike in the obvious things, Sylvie and I. But then, true friendship does not concern itself with the obvious."

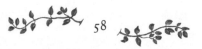

58

Sylvie said slowly: "You were my grandmother's true friend, then." She had a sense that the world had spun and opened around her; become wider, full of unknowns. She remembered that moment when she had held Grand-mère Sylvie's hand and had a tiny peek into her grandmother's unknown past.

"Yes," said Ceciline. "I was Sylvie's true friend. And now I will be yours." Unexpectedly, she stepped closer and cupped Sylvie's face in her palms. They were eye to eye. Sylvie held her breath. This woman pulsed with knowledge. Sylvie could feel it.

And she had had Grand-mère Sylvie's friendship.

What did Ceciline see in Sylvie now? Would she somehow sense what Sylvie had done to Jeanne? Her own knowledge of it, forced aside for days, returned now like a knife in Sylvie's throat.

"My dear," said Ceciline gently. "Whatever it is, hadn't you better tell me?"

Sylvie burst into tears.

She never was able to fully recall the minutes that followed. The strength of Ceciline's arms guiding her to a seat. Soothing words, the sense of which

Sylvie could not quite take in. A shawl wrapped about her, a tisane to drink, pressed into her hands. Martin hovering somewhere nearby, both embarrassed and concerned, deferring with obvious relief to Ceciline.

The miracle of being cared for once more; of not being alone, or responsible. Oh, the kind landlady at the inn had offered care, but only because of a misunderstanding and Sylvie's implicit lies. That mismatch made it even more of a relief for Sylvie to set down her burden of worry now.

She wondered if perhaps Ceciline might be the very teacher Sylvie sought, even if she had not read Sylvie's mind just now.

"Thank you," Sylvie said, when she could. She wiped away her tears and sat up straight.

She looked at Ceciline, and then at Martin. She began to apologize, but Ceciline cut her off with a wave of her hand.

"*La politesse* is not important or necessary," said Ceciline. "Not for us." She smiled wryly. "I never cared for polite rules, in any case, as your grandmother could have told you. Did she speak of me ever? Not at all? Well, Sylvie was always one to keep

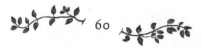

her focus on the present. It is clear that she led a full life after we parted, and that is happy news at least.

"And yet you cry, Sylvie, so all is not well. What has happened?" Ceciline had pulled a chair close to Sylvie; Martin's stool was also nearby. Sylvie felt both sets of eyes on her. "It's best that you talk about it." Ceciline's tone was firm, but not unkind.

Involuntarily, Sylvie glanced at Martin.

"You called him your friend," said Ceciline, who seemed only to need half the explanations that other people did. Her voice was almost reproving.

"Yes, but he's a child," Sylvie said doubtfully. "I should never have let him come with me to Montigny—"

Martin interrupted, his voice fierce and hurt. "It had nothing to do with you! I decided! She told me I might go with you if I liked, when the time came for you to leave, and I decided to." He met Sylvie's incredulous stare defiantly and added: "And don't ever talk about me like I'm not here. I am here." He scowled. "Me."

Sylvie was speechless.

Ceciline said quietly, "Who said you might go with Sylvie, Martin?"

"She did." Martin calmed as Ceciline visibly accepted his words. "Grand-mère Sylvie." Then he shrank a little on his stool, anxious, stealing a look at Sylvie. "She said I could call her that. She really did."

"I believe you," said Ceciline. But Martin was looking at Sylvie.

Sylvie's thoughts were as snarled as a dropped spindle. "I don't understand," she said finally. "Grand-mère Sylvie talked to you"—she managed to swallow the words *to a child*—"about *me*? She told you I would be leaving Bresnois? She told you to come with me?"

"If I chose," corrected Martin. "She said she had a vision of you leaving one day. She said she saw me with you. But she also said visions were only possibilities, and though she hoped I would go with you, it was up to me to choose." He paused. "Last spring, it was. We talked then. For a long time."

"Oh," said Sylvie. Last spring? So, then. A full year before Sylvie had known about her gift, her grandmother had had one of her rare visions. She pressed a hand to her head. She looked at Ceciline, who was watching the two of them with great

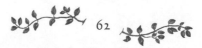

62

interest. She managed to grasp one of the questions whirling through her mind and ask it. "Martin? Did she tell you why I would have to go?"

"She didn't know. She just saw you leaving," said Martin baldly. He was visibly regaining confidence. "But when I saw you walking away that morning, I thought that this was probably it. Something about how you were walking. I can't explain it. So I went after you." He added, as if he felt the point needed still more emphasis: "Because I decided to."

Sylvie buried her head in her hands for a moment. She thought, why? Why Martin? Why would Grand-mère Sylvie want to send a child with her?

She heard Martin say to Ceciline, with a hint of bravado in his voice: "Grand-mère Sylvie said I'm a special person."

"I have always made a point of paying close attention to whomsoever my friend Sylvie found worthy of attention," said Ceciline.

CHAPTER
Eight

Then Ceciline said, "But the young Sylvie has not told us what is troubling her." She turned to Sylvie. "It's why you left home, isn't it?"

Sylvie gathered herself. "Yes." She looked at Martin, and then away. She would think about Martin's connection with Grand-mère Sylvie later.

Ceciline was nodding. "I thought so. And perhaps it is also the reason that Sylvie—your grand-mère—felt you would need Martin with you. I speculate."

"I don't know," said Sylvie. She took a deep breath. "I just know what I have done." She dared look straight at Ceciline: an appeal. "I need your help."

"I'll help you if I can," said Ceciline calmly. "As will Martin. We are your friends." Sylvie saw Martin nod; even in her distress she noted his shy pride at being included. "But first," Ceciline was saying, "you must tell us what has happened."

"I know," said Sylvie slowly.

Ceciline was silent. Martin, too, was attentive. Waiting. And so Sylvie fixed her eyes in her lap and began. It was more than the tale of what had happened on the day she hurt Jeanne. It had begun long before that.

Grand-mère Sylvie and Jeanne had raised Sylvie to be a healer, just as they—in their different ways— were. From when she was small, Sylvie was allowed to watch when someone came to the cottage with an ailment or complaint. Jeanne explained to her daughter exactly what should go into a poultice, or how to stop bleeding, or what to do to bring down a fever. Jeanne had endless knowledge of simples, and endless concern and patience too. While she had originally learned the healing arts from her own mother, Jeanne had in time far surpassed her in the ways of ordinary healing.

But there were times when ordinary healing was not sufficient.

"The ones that Jeanne could not help—they were for my grandmother," said Sylvie. "She could . . ." Sylvie paused, unable to find words. Grand-mère had never spoken of it directly, and neither had the villagers ever put anything into words. She looked up, helplessly, at Ceciline, who was nodding.

"She could lay hands to heal sometimes," said Ceciline. "A rare gift."

"Yes, her gift from God," said Sylvie.

Ceciline said, "And oh, how I envied her it, when I was young and foolish. It was wondrous to see."

Sylvie nodded in solemn agreement. She remembered the first time she had seen it. She told them.

Jeanne had helped Françoise, the miller's wife, through the difficult birth of an eighth child. The child had been large and lusty, but two days afterward, Françoise still lay wasting with a puerperal fever. And so Grand-mère Sylvie had come, bringing Sylvie. She had been six.

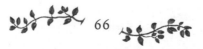

Françoise's husband, and all the children save the eldest daughter, had been sent from the room. Sylvie and the daughter had wrung out soft cloths in cool water and handed them to Jeanne, who gently washed Françoise's body, cooling her fever somewhat. But the room was filled with Françoise's low mutterings and moans. "If it's my time, then it's my time," she said once, almost with relief, before falling back into incoherence.

Then Jeanne had stepped back. Sylvie had felt her hands on her shoulders and looked up to see Jeanne's face, filled with an odd longing. She had followed her gaze.

Grand-mère Sylvie knelt on the pallet beside Françoise and was staring intently into her sweating, pain-filled face. She held her hands suspended in midair, flexing them.

Then she lowered them to Françoise's forearms, closed her eyes, and began to stroke, slowly, blindly, pressing on Françoise's arms.

Grand-mère Sylvie's forehead broke out in sweat, matching Françoise's. She said nothing. Sylvie felt Jeanne's hands bite into her shoulders. She watched Grand-mère Sylvie sway, holding

Françoise, touching her. Both of them covered in sweat now. Dripping.

"Françoise," said Grand-mère Sylvie. Her voice was low, singsong. Sylvie had to strain to hear it. "Françoise, you are loved. Françoise, you are needed. Françoise, Françoise. Stay, Françoise. Stay."

For how long this went on, Sylvie did not know. But then: "No!" shouted Françoise distinctly, the single word completely discernible. "No. Tired. So tired."

"Françoise, you are loved. Françoise, you are needed . . ."

". . . tired . . ."

"Françoise, you must stay. Choose to stay . . . choose."

And finally, Grand-mère Sylvie straightened her back and opened her eyes. Françoise lay still now, no longer moaning. Her eyes, which had been glassy with fever, fixed themselves on Grand-mère Sylvie's face. They were exhausted but clear. Then she sighed and closed them again, turning her face away. Her chest fell up and down evenly.

"She'll sleep now," said Grand-mère Sylvie. Her

voice was the merest thread; she had to clear her throat twice to make any sound emerge at all.

"Will she be all right?" asked Françoise's daughter. Throughout, she had sat still as a sheaf of wheat.

"Yes, I think so," said Grand-mère Sylvie. "If she has plenty of rest, and time. You will all need to help her, my dear. You and your father and your brothers and sisters. If you want to keep her, then, as much as you can, you must help her. Life has been . . . heavy for her."

"We will," said the girl earnestly. "I'm almost eleven. I can take care of the baby and the little ones. I can cook."

Grand-mère Sylvie sighed. "I know you can," she said to the girl, who nodded with purpose and began right then to pick up around the room. Grand-mère Sylvie's eyes followed her determined little body for a few moments. She shook her head and her lips moved as if she would say something else to the girl. But she did not. Instead she reached to pat Françoise's unconscious hand and stood up.

"I must go home now," she said. "I must rest. Jeanne?"

69

"I'll stay here for a while longer," said Sylvie's mother. "Sylvie can go with you and support you."

Sylvie left with her grand-mère to begin the walk home. She felt the heaviness with which Grand-mère Sylvie leaned on her as they walked. And after a time, she said, "Grand-mère? You took Françoise's fever away when you touched her?"

For a while she thought that Grand-mère Sylvie was not going to reply. But then she said, "I eased it a little, yes. But that is not so important." Grand-mère Sylvie stopped, right in the road. She knelt down and looked with her tired eyes right into Sylvie's. "I gave her some of my will, to strengthen her. Marriage can be hard on women. It can break us, in body and spirit both. Even with a good and loving man like the miller."

Sylvie nodded. She thought she understood. It was women who bore children, after all, and sometimes they came one after another after another after another, as with Françoise. "But you made Françoise better."

"Yes, I think so," said Grand-mère Sylvie. "For while I can sometimes heal the body with my will, my gift works even better when it is about healing

both the mind and the body. Sometimes, though not always, they are connected in illness, as with Françoise today."

"Oh," said Sylvie. She thought. "Maman cannot do what you can," she said. "Use her will to heal mind or body."

"No," said Grand-mère Sylvie. "She cannot. She would like to, but she cannot. It is just a fact." She stood up and brushed off her skirt. She began walking again. Sylvie rushed to catch up, to give Grand-mère Sylvie her shoulder. She knew she should say nothing more; she knew Grand-mère Sylvie was weary. But she could not stop herself from saying what she suddenly knew.

She said, simply, "One day, I will be able to heal like you do."

And Grand-mère Sylvie said: "Perhaps. Yes. Your mother and I both think that may be so." She had smiled then.

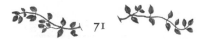

"Everyone knew about Grand-mère Sylvie," Martin said. "And that Jeanne was not like her. And everyone wondered about you, Sylvie."

Ceciline was leaning forward, intent. "So,

Sylvie? You can lay hands as well? Do you have visions as well?"

Sylvie found herself being evasive. "I have not done very much." She explained about having only recently come to womanhood and into a sense of her new gift. "But Grand-mère Sylvie asked me to be patient and not to use it."

"Why was that, did she say?"

"Because—because she felt I would need help to use my gift properly."

"Why?"

"Because—because . . ." There was really no sense in being vague, Sylvie realized. The words came out steadily after all. "You see, when I"—she fumbled for the phrase Ceciline had used—"when I lay hands on people, I can sense things in their minds. Read their minds, or their emotions, or parts of them."

Ceciline was staring, clearly fascinated. "As if the mind were a book?"

"No, it's more like pictures." Sylvie lifted her hands and then dropped them. "It's hard to describe."

"You know what people are thinking."

"Yes. If I touch them, and—and if I look. I don't

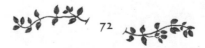

have to look. But I can." She added, compelled, "Have you ever heard of anything like this?"

After a long moment, Ceciline nodded.

"You have? But you—oh, you can't do this yourself." Sylvie, disappointed, read the answer in Ceciline's sweet, regretful smile.

"No," said Ceciline smoothly. "I cannot." There was a furrow in the middle of her forehead. She tilted her head. "But you haven't finished, have you, Sylvie?"

Sylvie reminded herself that this was her grandmother's friend. And Martin, her own friend. She whispered, "I don't know—I don't know yet all that I can do. But sometimes I can—I can reach in and touch the pictures I see. I can—take things out. Like removing a splinter."

"You have done this very thing?" said Ceciline. Her face was utterly still.

"Yes," said Sylvie. She meant to say it quietly, but it burst from her like a cork. She took in a deep breath. Martin was listening closely, his eyes fixed on her face. Ceciline, too, was intent, entirely still and yet somehow also visibly tense. Sylvie turned back to the window, away from them. She would

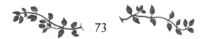

say all the rest. She would say it quickly, and it would be done.

"I told Grand-mère," Sylvie said. "I explained what I believed I could do. She said I should not actually try to do it. She said she could not help me with this, that we needed to find a teacher for me.

"But . . . but then she died, and Maman needed my help."

Jeanne had slumped like a rag doll without stuffing after Grand-mère had died. She had become someone else. Someone not strong at all. When people sent to the house for her, she did not go. If people came to her, she sent them away. She would not eat, or talk, or cry. And the days passed.

"I had to help her," said Sylvie to the plant on the windowsill. "Do you understand? I was only trying to help. I thought I could help her." She waited for Ceciline's voice, but it was Martin who spoke.

He said, wonderment in his voice: "Did you try to make her forget Grand-mère Sylvie, then?"

"No," said Sylvie sharply. "No! I don't remember now exactly what I thought I was doing. I held her shoulders, and I looked in her mind. I saw a mass of black and gray, pressing down. I took it out. I didn't

know what it was, exactly. I just . . . took it *out*."

"It was her grief," said Ceciline softly.

Sylvie swallowed. "Yes. But . . . it was not just her grief. It was me, too. And Grand-mère Sylvie. We were in there, somewhere in that black and gray. Because when I took it out, my mother had no memory of either of us."

She turned and faced them then. "Do you understand?" she said. "My mother did not know me! It was as if she had never had a daughter at all! She offered me a meal. She thought I was another healer on a journey, come to stay for a day or so." Sylvie stopped. "So I left," she said finally. "I left her."

Martin said tentatively: "Couldn't you have just put it back?"

Sylvie's fingers curled into claws. Then she straightened them. It was not Martin's fault. He was small. He knew nothing of all this, despite his talks with Grand-mère Sylvie. "No," she said quite calmly. "I could not. I don't know how."

"When you took it out, where did you put it? Do you still have . . . it?" asked Martin curiously.

"It's not a real thing, Martin—" began Ceciline, but Sylvie stopped her.

75

"But it is," she said to Ceciline. "And I do still have it." She put one hand to her head.

She probed gently with her mind and then flinched. "Here," she said. "I have it in here. And now . . . I need to find out more about my gift, so that I can fix my mother. And—not do harm again. My grandmother said, God gives us our gifts so that we will use them for good. Only I don't know how. It seems that I only know how to do harm! I left home because I am looking for help."

She stopped.

Ceciline sucked in a breath. "Oh," she said after a time.

Sylvie sighed. There was no more to say. No. There was one more thing to say. To ask. She looked at Ceciline and prepared to ask it. But Ceciline got up and held out both hands. She came to Sylvie and took Sylvie's hands in hers. Her smile was lovely.

"Oh, child," she said. "You do not even need to ask. The spirit of your grandmother must have guided you here, to me. Of course I can help you, and I will."

CHAPTER
Nine

They stayed that night at Ceciline's, both of them, Martin and Sylvie.

Sylvie had thought to send Martin back to the inn with a message to relieve the landlady of her worry. But Martin had shaken his head mulishly. "I remain where you are," he said. Sylvie had not argued, aware that the landlady had not seemed to like or trust Ceciline and a message might equally cause trouble. And perhaps it was not really needed. Surely she would be too busy to fret overmuch about a girl she had met so briefly.

Besides, Sylvie was too tired to think about it

more. She barely had strength to taste the food Ceciline served them for an evening meal.

"We'll talk more in the morning," Ceciline said.

From the way she felt, Sylvie recognized that Ceciline must have given her something to help her sleep, but she did not care; she knew it was meant kindly even though, vaguely, she thought that Ceciline ought to have told her. Jeanne always did in similar cases . . .

She slept, dreamless.

In the morning, Sylvie opened her eyes to face the whitewashed beams of the loft roof and found herself alone. Below, she could hear movement and soft voices. Martin and Ceciline. She thought momentarily of the hustle and bustle of the inn and again brushed away guilt over the landlady. She washed her face and feet in a basin and went down the ladder as slowly and cautiously as if her bones were made of precious glass.

Ceciline was seated at the table, writing with a feather pen on a piece of rag paper. Martin stood leaning over her shoulder, watching the movement of the pen so closely that Sylvie wondered Ceciline could work at all. But Ceciline did not seem to mind.

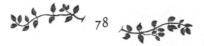

She paused from time to time to dip the pen in an inkwell. Then she would wipe off the excess ink and resume writing as Martin watched—with great interest, Sylvie thought. Like most village children, he had not been offered the opportunity to learn his letters. Perhaps Sylvie could teach him sometime, she thought, if Martin wished.

Beneath Ceciline's hand the words flowed in a tiny, careful stream, reminding Sylvie reassuringly of Grand-mère Sylvie's equally painstaking literacy. Ceciline finished one letter, slowly, frowning a little to herself, and then began another, much shorter one. Finally she put down the pen, shook sand over the page to fix the ink on the second letter, looked up, and smiled good morning at Sylvie.

"I'm writing to my friend Robert," she explained. "He is young and energetic and trustworthy. I have undertaken to ask him to bring you—both of you—to a woman in Lyon who can help you."

Sylvie was surprised, even shocked. Lyon! After Paris, it was the biggest city in France, and located far to the east and south. She had never imagined going that far from Bresnois. She did not want to. But she thought of her mother and bit her lip.

Martin was ecstatic: "Lyon! Sylvie, think of it!" He turned to Ceciline. "You're sure this Robert person will take us? Really?"

"Yes," Ceciline said, and smiled crookedly. "I am quite certain he will." She folded the paper she had written and sealed it. "He travels often on business, and is about to set off, and had planned a stop in Lyon in any case. This letter asks him to take the both of you to Madame du Bois, the one I know of who will help you, Sylvie. He will do it as a favor to me."

Sylvie asked, "But why do I need *her*, this Madame du Bois? I thought I had found *you*." She made a gesture.

"I cannot help you in this provincial place," said Ceciline seriously. "It is not wise. There would inevitably be talk. Trust me."

Sylvie remembered again the landlady's suspicion of Ceciline. Reluctantly, she nodded.

"But never fear. You will see me again, in Lyon." Ceciline was smiling again. "You're Sylvie's granddaughter. I would never abandon you."

Martin's face was already alight with the joy of adventure. He reached for the first letter and held it

in both hands, eyes scanning it as carefully as if he could read, as reverently as if it were a sacred relic. "Lyon!" he repeated, his voice caressing the word.

"Tell me of this Madame du Bois," Sylvie said to Ceciline.

"She is a woman of importance in Lyon," said Ceciline. "And a good friend of mine. She is knowledgeable and will advise you well." She reached across the table and picked up the second letter. "This is for her." She held out the letter to Sylvie.

Sylvie wanted to be told that everything could be put back the way it had been. That Jeanne would remember her and Grand-mère Sylvie. She wanted the impossible, too; she wanted Grand-mère Sylvie back again. Going far away seemed wrong.

But Ceciline's offer of help was all she had.

She took up the letter. *Madame du Bois*, it said. *Croix-Rousse. Lyon.*

"Robert will take you to her," said Ceciline gently. She took the other letter away from Martin and handed it also to Sylvie. "That one is for Robert, to explain," Ceciline said. "I will give you directions to his house. It is right here in Montigny. You will go now to him with the letter, yes?"

81

Sylvie read the name on this letter. She blinked. Then she read it a second time. It said the same thing: *Monsieur Robert Chouinard.*

Monsieur Chouinard.

Sylvie looked from the letter to Martin's excited face. He had seen the letter, but of course he could not read. Out loud, Ceciline had called her friend only by the name *Robert*. Yet it was clear: Ceciline's friend and the owner of the blue surcoat, the merchant who employed Yves the accountant, were one and the same. So: the arrogant rich young man, whom she had thought to never see again—Ceciline proposed that they travel all the way to Lyon under his protection.

Could Martin bear it? For that matter, could she? But then again, what choice was there?

Sylvie decided abruptly; her entire life was on the line here. She would do what Ceciline asked. She would give this Monsieur Robert Chouinard the letter. She would leave whatever happened as a result up to God.

Where it belonged.

"Yes," she said.

82

Martin skipped happily along beside Sylvie as they retraced their steps to the inn. They had left Sylvie's pack there; more, she was anxious to apologize to the kindly landlady for not having returned the previous evening. And it was too early in the morning in any case, she told Martin, to disturb Ceciline's friend Robert.

Robert was what Martin called Monsieur Chouinard in his excited chatter. Ceciline had told him much about Robert, it seemed, before Sylvie was awake. She knew Martin's new hero worship would last no longer than his first glimpse of Robert's face.

She needed to warn Martin in advance. But she hesitated to interrupt his happiness. Let him have this brief time, she thought—and let her not have to handle his reaction until she had at least managed her own feelings.

Lyon. It was unimaginably far from home. Far from Jeanne.

They reached the inn. Sylvie caught just a glimpse of the landlady's relieved face before she was enveloped in a huge, warm embrace. "Thanks be to God," said the landlady. "You're all right. I lay

awake all night—I thought of sending my husband to look for you, but he told me to wait. I was going to go myself, later this morning, once I had our guests fed. Thanks be, thanks be!"

It was the warmest embrace Sylvie had known since her grandmother's death. Ceciline's arms had been strong but cool. She felt the tears start in her eyes. How wrong she had been to think the land-lady would have forgotten her!

"I'm well," she said. "I'm sorry you were wor-ried. We stayed the night at Ceciline's. I apologize. I should have sent a message. I apologize, my dear madame."

"You stayed there?" The landlady stepped back.

"Yes," said Sylvie. She found herself speaking rapidly as, wanting to make up for her evasions before, she tried to explain. "I'm afraid I misled you yesterday. I wasn't—that is, I just needed to talk with a wisewoman. And it turned out that Ceciline was a friend of my grandmother's, you see, and I—"

"Friend? But you didn't know her," said the land-lady. Her face had gone quite still. "I had to tell you Ceciline's name yesterday. I had to tell you where she lived."

"That's right, I was only looking for a healer, a wisewoman like—"

"Like your grandmother?" interrupted the landlady. "Your grandmother was like Ceciline?"

Sylvie nodded, uneasy at the change she could sense in the landlady, but determined now to be truthful. "Yes . . ."

"And like you," said the landlady, in a voice suddenly cold as clay. It was not a question. "I understand now," she said.

"Sylvie," said Martin. He had stepped up beside her. He had her pack strapped on his sturdy little back. He was watching the landlady too. He tugged at Sylvie's arm. "Let's go, Sylvie," he said. "Let's get out of here."

"Do as the boy tells you," said the landlady. "This is a Christian place." Her voice rose. "A Christian place!"

"But please," Sylvie said. "I'm Christian. Believe me, I am sorry that I—"

"Get out!" screamed the landlady. "Get out! You! You are a witch like her! You—" She screamed terrible things. She screamed words that Sylvie had never heard before, but which she did not have to

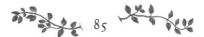

know to understand. She screamed things about Ceciline, horrible things, things even worse than *witch*, things no one had said in Bresnois about Grand-mère Sylvie, because it was a small village, Bresnois. Because they had a place there. Because Grand-mère Sylvie had made them a place there, before Sylvie was even born. Because Jeanne was loved there. Because people understood there. Because people were not like the landlady there.

Were they?

With Martin beside her, Sylvie walked out of the inn. The terrible words faded away behind her, but she knew she would never forget them.

Nor would she ever forget the landlady, who had gone so swiftly from indifference to caring and now to hatred. She had given Sylvie no space to explain. She had given herself no space to ask for or consider new ideas.

Grand-mère Sylvie had warned her.

Thank God she had found Ceciline, Sylvie thought miserably.

CHAPTER

Ten

"Forget her," said Martin after they had walked a quarter mile back toward the center of town. "That hag doesn't know anything. She reminds me of the miller's wife, back in Bresnois. You never knew where you were with her, either. One minute smiling, next minute yelling. I hate people like that."

Martin was a sweet boy, Sylvie thought. He didn't fully understand what had just happened, but he was trying to comfort her. That was something. It was quite a lot.

"Besides, we have things to do," Martin was

saying. "We should go see Robert right now. I don't think it's too early. What if he leaves today? We don't want him to go without us!"

Sylvie pulled herself together. Martin was right; Monsieur Chouinard was more important than the landlady. And Martin . . . was more important than either. Ready or not, she had to warn him of what lay ahead. She pulled him to the side of the road, made him put down her pack and sit on it. She took out the letter Ceciline had written and pointed to the letters that formed the name Chouinard and spelled them out for him.

"It's him, Martin," she concluded. "It must be. The merchant from the market. Monsieur Chouinard. Ceciline's friend. They are the same man."

Martin was still staring at the letters she had pointed out as if, by the force of his gaze, he could turn them into a different name. Disbelief, protest, flared before dying in his eyes. He slumped, his dirty knees tucked up close to his chin.

She said, "Yet we have to go with him—if he'll have us, that is."

"We could go to Lyon ourselves," said Martin.

 88

"We got here on our own, didn't we? Why do we need *him*?"

Sylvie sat down next to Martin. "It's a long way to Lyon, and dangerous. There are mountains and robbers. And we haven't much money." She paused.

"Ceciline might give us some money," said Martin.

"I won't ask her," said Sylvie. "She's done enough for us. She has done what she thinks is best. And she does not look rich." Martin was silent.

"*I* need to go, Martin. But you could still go home," Sylvie offered, though the moment she said it, she knew she could not bear to think of Martin traveling home alone.

With that, Martin looked up. "No," he said. He stood. "I'm staying with you. Chouinard or no Chouinard."

Sylvie nodded, relieved.

The egg-boy was correct, Sylvie thought, when they found Monsieur Chouinard's house. It was big. Grand. Even from where they stood, outside the front door, facing a servant's sneer, she could see the edge of a rich blue carpet where it lay upon a polished wood floor. The elegantly turned leg of a chair. The servant's supercilious eye swept her, and Sylvie was uncomfortably aware of her dress, old and patched and inches too short. She blushed. But she said again, obstinately: "Monsieur Chouinard will see us. I have a letter for him."

"I will take mademoiselle's letter to Monsieur," said the servant smoothly, reaching.

Sylvie didn't trust the servant to deliver it. She whipped the letter behind her back. "I have to give it to him in person."

The servant shrugged and shut the door in their faces. Sylvie exchanged a glance with Martin. He shrugged; the gesture was a near-perfect imitation of the servant's. Then he sat down on the stairs, his face set in the stubborn cast that Sylvie knew well. After a moment, she sat down beside him and stored the letter in the pocket she wore tied around her waist.

On the clean, whitewashed steps, they waited. They waited through the appearance of three other servants of varying rank up to maître d'hôtel, all come to urge and then threaten them away. Sylvie followed Martin's lead and remained silent. They

waited through the arrival of several businessmen, all of whom stepped carefully around Martin and Sylvie as if they were dung. They waited as the sun rose high in the sky, and people passed in the street, and then repassed. They waited until the first servant finally opened the door and said between compressed lips: "Monsieur Chouinard will see you."

Sylvie got up immediately, feeling her legs protest at having been too long in one position. Martin got up more deliberately. He made the servant, holding the door, wait until he had stretched fully. Then he strolled in behind Sylvie. Oh, Martin, please, Sylvie thought. But she could say nothing.

They were shown into a small room off the spacious entry hall. In it was a desk, and behind the desk sat Robert Chouinard, and in his face sat the same pair of sharp eyes that she knew from the market. They were old eyes in a young face, and they recognized her and Martin at once, but did not express surprise or curiosity or, indeed, anything at all.

No one said a word about the egg or offered any kind of greeting.

"You have a letter for me?" Robert said, and

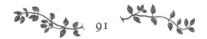

Sylvie handed it over almost before she realized she had taken it from her pocket. She watched as he broke the seal and read it. He looked up after a short time. She saw him note Martin's defiant stance, but then his gaze rested on her face.

"So, then," said Robert Chouinard conversationally. "You know Ceciline."

"She was a friend of my"—Sylvie glanced at Martin—"of *our* grandmother." It was unfair, she thought. He was seated comfortably while they stood here before him like supplicants.

"Ah," he said.

She blurted: "What does Ceciline say in the letter? May I see it?"

"Oh, can you read?" he asked, looking mildly surprised.

Sylvie nodded tightly. He handed the letter to her. She began to read it to herself and then, remembering Martin, began again at the beginning. It was quite short.

"'My dear Robert,'" she read aloud. "'Sylvie and Martin need to visit Madame du Bois in Lyon. I am sure you will be so kind as to escort them to her.'" Sylvie looked up, relieved that Ceciline had

not revealed anything personal. Indeed, the letter was peculiarly curt in tone. Perhaps, despite what Ceciline had said, Ceciline and Robert were not truly friends?

"Well, then," she said. "Will you take us?"

"Certainly," said Robert Chouinard, without expression. "Since Ceciline has asked." And as Sylvie frowned, confused, he added: "Our party will be twenty persons, with you two included. We leave tomorrow." Once more, his eyes swept them comprehensively, and this time he was the one to frown.

"That boy," he said to Sylvie, "will need shoes."

Eleven

"I don't want them," said Martin. He was sitting on the ground, one foot half-booted, one bare. He held up the empty right boot to Sylvie, and she took it. Concentrating, pulling, he finally managed to get the first boot onto his left foot. He stared at it. "It pinches," he said.

Sylvie looked at the second boot in her hand and then at his foot. "They'll stretch with use," she said hopefully. Her own sturdy shoes had been made last year by the Bresnois shoemaker in payment for Jeanne nursing his eldest son back to health. They had fit correctly from the start. They still did.

Whereas Martin's boots—well, they had obviously been fitted to someone else. Who had given up their boy-child's new boots? Sylvie wondered. Someone rich enough to buy such boots, but not rich enough to refuse Robert Chouinard.

Martin began pushing at the boot on his left foot. He grabbed at the heel with both hands and shoved. "I won't wear them. I don't need them," he said. His hands slipped on the stiff new leather. He looked as if he were going to cry.

Sylvie gazed helplessly around the bustling caravan area. No one was paying any attention at all to them. It was only just after dawn; sturdy pack-horses were being hitched to wagons, taller, prouder horses being mounted. In the distance Sylvie saw Robert—no, Monsieur Chouinard, that was how she wished to think of him. He was listening impassively to one of his men, one hand absently stroking the nose of a magnificent brown mare.

They were to leave Montigny within minutes. The accountant Yves, who was also second-in-command of the caravan, had arrived before dawn and found them waiting, shivering, uncertain. Having nowhere else to go, they had spent the

 95

night there. Yves had eyed them up and down, without a word making it clear that he considered himself too important to be bothered with them. Yet he had brought the boots for Martin, no doubt on Monsieur Chouinard's orders. He had pointed toward the wagon in which they were to travel, advised them with a curl of the lip to "stay out of the way," and rushed off.

"Come on," said Sylvie, gesturing toward the wagon now. "Let's get in, and I'll help you take the boot off. You won't need boots while we're riding, anyway." Grimacing, Martin limped to the wagon and let her help him up into the back with the cargo. She settled him on a soft pile of tapestry rolls and managed to pull off the offending boot. The driver turned, noted their presence, but responded with only a nod to Sylvie's cautious smile. His eyes examined her thoroughly, though, so that she had to look away.

There were twenty people on the expedition, but Sylvie was the only female. And she was no lady to be granted automatic courtesy. She would be careful, she thought sturdily. Very careful. Again, she looked for Monsieur Chouinard. Ceciline had

trusted him to protect them. Sylvie, too, would have to do so. Was doing so.

She wished desperately for her mother. For Grand-mère Sylvie. For Ceciline. But what she had was Martin, rubbing his foot, following her gaze to Monsieur Chouinard.

"I still don't like him," said Martin truculently, as if he had been asked.

Sylvie said, "I know. Just keep any eggs to yourself."

That gained her, at least, his brief grin. "Maybe."

The sun rose higher. One of the guards raised a horn to his lips and blew it: one, two, three blasts. The wagons, the horses, formed into a line. With a deliberateness that felt almost anticlimactic, the party headed out of town and turned to the southeast. The wagon in which Sylvie and Martin rode jounced along the ruts in the road. And jounced. After a while Martin put his head down in Sylvie's lap and slept. She wondered how he could.

There was much to see, if she could ignore the bone-rattling bouncing. The fields stretched out on either side of the road, and Sylvie's height on the wagon afforded a vista not possible on foot. The

hills beyond. The wildflowers and herbage bloom-ing by the side of the road and visible sometimes in brief flashes of color between fields. Some Sylvie did not recognize and would have liked to inves-tigate. But she knew better than to ask. This was a business trip, and men did not stop for flowers and herbs. It made Sylvie a little uneasy; they were a large party—what if someone were injured, got sick, and she needed to help them? Would the small amount she carried now be enough? But then, she told herself, their health was not her responsibility. She was not her mother. She did not need to care for every sick creature who stumbled in her way; nor would she be expected to.

These people knew nothing about her, and that was best. It was; it truly was. She pulled her eyes from the land around them and focused on the car-avan and the men.

She counted eight wagons of varying sizes, pulled by teams. Of the horsebacked men, a large number looked like soldiers: leathery, hard-eyed. Mercenaries. The accountant and aide-de-camp Yves sweated beneath an inappropriately chosen

velvet doublet, and spent the miles cantering offi-
ciously from front to back, back to front, talking first
with one person and then with another. Her lips
curved. How could the man possibly have so much
to communicate, only two hours from Montigny?

A quiet voice said: "You are amused?"

Sylvie shaded her eyes with her hand. It was
Robert Chouinard, drawing his horse up to walk
alongside their wagon. In her lap, Martin did not stir.

"You were watching Yves and smiling. He
amuses you?" said the merchant.

She fumbled for words that would not be dis-
courteous. "It's just . . . he seems very busy."

"Yes, he'll wear himself out before the week
ends. He's still new to my employ, you see. I hired
him because he knows Italian double-entry bookkeeping, which I am keen to use. But on this trip,
Yves needs to make himself useful in other ways as
well. He is eager to do so."

Sylvie nodded politely. She stole a glance
around and had the impression—oddly, because in
fact no one was looking at them directly—that the
attention of the entire party was upon them. Yves

cantered by again, ostentatiously not looking at them and managing to stir up even more dust on the road. Sylvie coughed.

"Very well," said Monsieur Chouinard reflectively. "I'll have a talk with him. Perhaps I can settle him down. He's not so bad, really, you know. Ambitious, which is actually good."

About this, Sylvie kept her own counsel.

The road had turned, and trees now blocked the sun so that she could see the young merchant's face. He was looking at her expectantly. For what? And why should he care what she thought about Yves? Why was he talking to her at all? She said gravely, "That would be fine," and fancied he looked disappointed.

"It has occurred to me," Monsieur Chouinard said, "that in spite of our—interesting—first few meetings, we have yet to make formal acquaintance." He swept off his hat and made her an elegant bow from the horse's back. "Robert Chouinard. My trade and position you know. And you are?"

"Sylvie. Just Sylvie." There was no need for a last name in Bresnois; everyone knew them. "Oh, and my . . . my brother, Martin." She stroked Martin's

hair gently. Did Monsieur Chouinard's eyes sharpen at her hesitation? No matter. She added, to cover her gaffe: "We are from Bresnois. It's—"

But he was nodding in recognition. "A village some sixty miles east of Montigny?"

She was surprised. "You know it? It's small."

"I have heard of it in passing." An ironic stretch of the lips; not a smile, and not even directed at her, but, somehow, inward. He added: "I have a habit of remembering what I hear."

Sylvie believed him. She said, "Well, there is nothing to attract a merchant in Bresnois. We don't even have a lord. At least, there is one, but he lives far away. He is not interested in us."

A skeptical eyebrow now. "Even at tax time?"

She blushed. "Oh, then, of course. He sends a collector. Last year we gave him a pair of our best hens." Now she was babbling. He made her feel gauche, stupid.

"We?"

Sylvie stiffened. She could see now; he was fishing for information. And she had things to hide . . . but not this, surely? She said slowly: "My grandmother, my mother, and I."

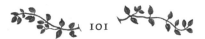

"Ah. Your grandmother, who knows Ceciline."

"Yes." Sylvie's stomach tightened. Thank God, she thought, that Martin was still sleeping. He would like these questions even less than she did.

Monsieur Chouinard pressed on. "Tell me about your grandmother."

Now. She would stop this now. Sylvie looked Monsieur Chouinard right in the eye and said: "She's dead." And had the satisfaction of having, for once, taken him aback.

But only for a moment. His eyes flickered, and then he said: "I have offended you, I see, with my questions. I apologize."

The words were apologetic, but the tone was not. She said, "I am not offended," though she was not sure if she was or not. She did not know what was safe to say and what was not. Ceciline, she reminded herself. Ceciline trusts this man. She added impulsively: "I think I don't really believe, yet, that she's gone. I try to imagine what advice she would give me, were she here."

"Is that a good thing?" said Monsieur Chouinard. "That you imagine her here?"

Sylvie's chin jerked up. "Yes," she said. "Of course it is!"

His eyes were narrow on her face. He said, surprising Sylvie: "I believe you." Then he said: "Would you permit one more question?" Without waiting for her to reply, he continued: "How long have you known Ceciline yourself?"

Sylvie said, "I have just met her, but she was a friend of my grandmother's. That's all I need to know." She lifted her chin, and added: "And you? How do you know her?"

He hesitated before saying: "I met her when I was not much older than your brother Martin, who is awake, I believe. And listening." He nodded quite politely to Martin, who sat up abruptly and was almost thrown askew as the wagon hit a particularly deep rut in the road. Sylvie grabbed him.

"Is that true?" she asked. "Were you eavesdropping?"

"I wasn't hiding," Martin said defensively. "You knew I was here." He glared at Monsieur Chouinard. "I don't like you asking her—my sister—questions. You have questions, you ask me."

Sylvie hadn't cared for the questions, either, but there was no need for rudeness, or for an eight-year-old boy to think he needed to, or could, protect her. "Martin," she began.

But Monsieur Chouinard raised a hand and stopped her. "I think," he said, directly to Martin, "that all my questions have been answered." His gaze shifted to Sylvie, and he added: "At least for now." He doffed his hat again, punctiliously, and rode back toward the head of the caravan. And around them, again, Sylvie sensed the attention of the caravan, lingering on her and Martin. But what they thought she could not guess.

She said, "Martin. You will have to get along with him. It is only for a few weeks. It's important. At least you must be polite."

Martin turned his face away from her and did not answer.

CHAPTER
Twelve

Their travel was blessed by largely fair weather. Even the rain confined itself to nighttime and ended long enough before dawn to ensure that the roads were not too badly muddied. At night, Sylvie and Martin slept together on some coarse canvas beneath their wagon. Since Martin had long since entirely appropriated Grand-mère Sylvie's shawl, rolling himself up in it next to Sylvie, she was glad of the blanket that Yves allocated to them.

It was only the first of many "allocations." Everyone else, Sylvie soon saw, had brought their own provisions—from bowls for stew to ale and blankets and spoons. Robert Chouinard even had a peculiar little pronged stabbing instrument for eating that he called a fork. Only they, as "guests"—the word Monsieur Chouinard used to introduce and explain them—had little beyond what they were given. Sylvie realized that she'd had no idea what Ceciline's request would involve; how much debt it would accumulate and how much care it would require on Robert's part to conduct them such a distance safely. How could she have known?

Travel, before, had meant packing a few things and walking to where you wanted to go. It had not even distantly resembled this massive shifting of men and stores and equipment and *things*. Things! All the things they were transporting. Heavy bolts of cloth, linen and woolen, woven in Brussels. Crates of wine from Germany. Sugar from the Canary Islands, which had already traveled by Portuguese vessel up the Atlantic coast to the port of Bruges before coming overland to Montigny. And seven huge rolls of tapestries from Flanders, which largely occupied their own wagon and against which Sylvie and Martin leaned and bumped while they were in that wagon.

It was overwhelming for a girl who had under-

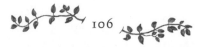

stood trade as the fact that you could exchange healing skill for a pair of shoes, a season's worth of mint leaves for a pig. It made her feel helpless to be suddenly dependent, in this alien mercantile world, upon the goodwill of a stranger. To understand that the goodwill, like everything else, must have a price, even if that price were not asked, or had been paid already by Ceciline. And, despite the unfailing (though distant) courtesy of Robert Chouinard, it was humiliating to be so dependent. In fact, Sylvie wondered if somehow, subtly, his courtesy—and that of his men, clearly following his lead—for some reason she could not name, made her feel worse. Martin seemed to think it was indeed humiliating; Sylvie had never seen Martin's new boots again.

Nor had Martin stayed in the wagon. The pace of the caravan, mandated by the hardworking packhorses and their loads, was slow enough to allow for long stretches of walking. In preference to the endless jolting of the wagon, Martin took to his feet, bare as they were. Soon enough, Sylvie joined him. And while Martin ran hither and yon almost as much as Yves, she was able to investigate the nearby grasses and vegetation. She gathered aloe for

crushing and took a rooted sample of some excellent soft mosses that could be bound in wounds. She felt better for having them. Jeanne always said, better extra than not enough.

Walking, surrounded by the bustling of the men but largely left alone to observe them and the landscape as it slowly changed, she began, warily, almost to enjoy the journey.

Martin, too, had gradually relaxed. After that first day he had regained a good deal of his normal cheerfulness. Within two or three days, he seemed to know everyone in the party. He chattered to the cook, volunteering cleanup duty in exchange for second helpings. He stole just enough sugar from stores to befriend the horses, from the humble strong pack animals to the taller mounts for riding. He did a wicked imitation of the bustling Yves, to the loud-voiced guffaws of the mercenaries and the cook. And he took, especially, to one of the merchants, a grizzled giant of a man called Arnaud. The liking was clearly mutual; Arnaud began to take Martin up pillion from time to time, and to save a place for Martin—and Sylvie—at meals. In fact, only when Martin spied Robert Chouinard did any

of his prickliness reappear. But this happened rarely; Robert tended to ride behind the mass of the party, or ahead, and to keep to himself at night. Sylvie was glad of this, for Martin's sake. She did not acknowledge any sense of disappointment in herself.

And no one asked questions, of her or of Martin.

"Ten days on the road," said Martin one evening, as they sat by the fire with Arnaud and two mercenaries. "You keep talking about robbers, and being careful, and keeping a sharp eye out, but I haven't seen a single one yet."

"Disappointed, boy?" Arnaud's laugh was like the bark of a big dog. "It's early days yet. We've got to stay prepared all the way to Marseille. Though it'll be easier after Lyon, once we're on the river."

"Why would someone rob our caravan?" Sylvie asked shyly. "It would need to be planned carefully, and there would need to be lots of them, and, well, they'd need to be prepared for a fight, surely?"

Arnaud stabbed a bit of meat with his knife, popped it into his mouth, and chewed it carefully. "Do you know what this cargo is worth, girl?" A rhetorical question, for he went right on without giving her time to answer, his strong yellow teeth

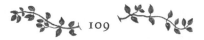

gleaming in the firelight. "Storms downed an entire fleet of sugar ships last winter, so the price of our sugar alone is . . ." He raised his palm above his head. "And half the linen was specially ordered by Florence." He lowered his voice confidentially on the last word. "It's the first time he's had direct dealings with *that* family, so you can bet he's anxious not to mess up." Arnaud did not specify who "he" was, but did not need to. Within the confines of the caravan party, the pronoun, used alone, always meant Robert Chouinard.

"What family? What's Florence?" asked Martin.

Arnaud sighed. "Boy, it's a good thing you're sharp, because you'll need it to make up for the ignorance." He grinned. Martin, clearly taking no offense, watched intently as Arnaud began to draw a map in the dirt with the tip of his knife. Sylvie leaned forward as well. "Here's France. And here, below us, there's the Mediterranean Sea." A sharp line intersected France to the sea. "The river Rhône," said Arnaud. "Meets the sea here, which is the direction where we're headed, to go down the river by barge and then on to Marseille by sea. I know you won't be with us after Lyon, but you'll

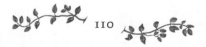

be interested anyway." The knife moved again in the dust, drawing a boot, below and to the right of France, beside the sea. "The Italian states. Venice." The knife paused briefly in economic respect. "Then all the way down here, Naples. Rome. Genoa. Savoy. Milan. And here"—Arnaud suddenly dug the knife right into the dirt and left it, hilt quivering— "Tuscany and its capital, Florence. Where whatever the de' Medici family wants is what matters. Because take my word for this: the only word you say to a de' Medici is *yes*." He laughed. "At least in public."

"But that family can't be more important than our king!" Martin, squinting at the dirt map, was scornful. "Look. France is four—five times as big!"

Arnaud laughed. "Weren't you listening? De' Medici. Why, two popes have been de' Medicis." And as Martin still looked blank, he added: "Power, boy. Power, money, experience. That family has been around for a long time, and you don't want to cross them. I could tell you tales about the de' Medicis that would curdle your blood. I guarantee, our king François knows them all. He's not in their league. Not yet, anyway." He added some more

wood chips to the fire, and it flared up brightly. "Plus," he said thoughtfully, almost longingly, "Paris is all well and good, but it's no Florence. There's this one artist—an architect, too—works in Florence for the de' Medicis. Buonarroti, his name is. Some people say they see God every day, but me, I see him while looking at this man's work."

Sylvie smiled to herself and shook her head. Why would you need man-made work to see God's hand? Weren't the living things of the earth enough?

Martin was oblivious to Arnaud's last comments. "Where is Paris?" he asked doggedly. Arnaud pulled out the knife and made a mark on the dirt map. "Montigny?" said Martin, and Arnaud made another mark. "Here." Then he put in Lyon and Nantes and Toulouse and Amiens and other cities he said were important and of which Sylvie and Martin had never heard. He put in Corsica and the Canary Islands. He put in Flanders and Luxembourg and Brabant and Burgundy and Hohenzollern and Cleves and Hesse. Martin leaned close and soaked up everything Arnaud said. He peppered the air with questions about the best way to get to Paris

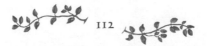

from Montigny, and why Frankish wine was prized, and who ruled where and how important they were to trade, which took Arnaud deep into a discussion of a current scandal involving the king of England, who was attempting to sweet-talk the pope into annulling his marriage. "After near twenty years and many children. True, only one girl has survived. Still, holy matrimony is holy matrimony. Should God's law bend for kings wanting heirs?" He raised his brows quizzically. "We all anxiously await the pope's decision."

"But the king's marriage won't affect trade," Martin objected.

Arnaud rolled his eyes at this naivete. "*Everything* affects trade, boy. Just look at this route on my map." He drew a line in the dust with the tip of his knife.

Sylvie tried to locate where Bresnois might be. It would not, she now understood, rate even so much as a speck on Arnaud's map. How will we get back there? she wondered. There would be no caravan escort, that was certain. Her head spun with the size of the world, and with tiredness, and with the

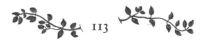

endless lilt of Martin's eager questions rising above the crackling of the fire. Martin likes it out here in the world, Sylvie thought, but I do not. At least, I do not think I do. Maybe that's why Grand-mère Sylvie wanted him to come with me.

"But where is this England?" asked Martin.

"Across the water—here, boy, you're nearer. Take up my knife, and you be the one to sketch it in. There, to the north and west." Arnaud pointed.

Martin obediently tugged at Arnaud's knife, which had been left stuck deep into the ground to mark the port of Calais. Dislodging it required some pulling. Martin gave one, two, three squatting, two-handed pulls. Then, on the fourth and last incautious, triumphant heave, Martin overbalanced himself. He squawked as he fell sideways and backward. He cast out one quick-witted hand to catch himself—and put that hand directly into the fire.

He screamed—*screamed*—

Arnaud got there before Sylvie could. He grabbed Martin and pulled him out. With his leathern coat, he crushed the fire on Martin's hand.

Everyone came running. Martin was sobbing now, dry sobs, kneeling on the ground, holding

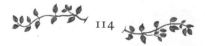

his hand out in disbelief. Arnaud had him around the shoulders, was supporting the forearm. Sylvie threw herself before Martin.

On Martin's right hand, the skin was already puckering, fingers swelling, red and black. It was bad. Sylvie knew at a glance. It was very bad.

She knelt by him. "Let me," she said to Arnaud, and took Martin's forearm gently, firmly.

"What in God's name—" she heard, and recognized Robert Chouinard's voice. She ignored him. She ignored them all as they crowded round.

"Sylvie," said Martin desperately, his voice high and frightened.

She held his eyes. "I'm here with you, Martin," she said firmly. It helped. She watched him work hard to calm himself, and succeed. The sobs slowed and stilled. But his whole body shook.

"The cook's got some skill," said Arnaud to her, low. The cook was stepping forward, wiping his hands on his apron. He had his big knife. Arnaud's brow was sweating. He said to Sylvie, "Girl, I've seen things. I tell you, it's best to just go ahead now and chop—"

"No. No! Leave us alone." Sylvie did not raise

her voice, but it stopped them all the same. It kept them back. For now.

Martin said her name again. His eyes met hers pleadingly, and she knew what he was asking of her. She knew it was impossible, that it was the wild fantasy of a hurt boy. But she answered anyway. "Yes," she said, though she knew with despair that even Grand-mère Sylvie could not have helped, not with this. "Shhh. Don't worry. I can help you," she said, because the impulse to comfort him was too strong to resist.

Jeanne *would* have been able to help. Sylvie knew exactly what she would have done. First, water to cleanse. Then aloe squeezed on the burns. Then nursing through the fever that would come, while saying the Lord's Prayer over and over. Only later, and only if need be, would Jeanne have had two big men hold Martin while she set her teeth and raised the ax. While she brought the ax down, accurately, herself. In this moment of need, Sylvie understood her mother's strength fully, for perhaps the first time. In this moment of need, Sylvie missed her more desperately than ever.

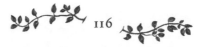

Yet she, too, was a healer, so she hoped. Jeanne was not here, but Sylvie was.

"I will try," Sylvie told Martin, though she thought he was now past being able to hear her. But he could see her. She drew Martin's eyes into hers. She held them, and as she did she reached down with her own hands and closed them on Martin's wounded one.

She heard the gasps, the stir, of the men. But Martin did not make a sound. She looked into him, and she thought of his beautiful quick hands that could pluck fish from a stream and eggs from the air. Carefully she formed his right hand in her mind, finger by finger. The chubby palm, graven across by a peculiarly broad lifeline. The dirty knuckles. Having formed a strong picture, she sent it slowly, strongly, down her neck and into her shoulders. Filling her chest. Then down her arms. She felt the picture now in her fingers that held Martin's. She held it there, solid and firm. Then she sent it into Martin. How much time passed, she did not know. She held on.

Aloud, she prayed, as Jeanne would have done.

"Pater noster, qui es in caelis, sanctificetur nomen tuum . . ."

"Sylvie," Martin whispered finally. "Let go. You're hurting me."

Her gaze flickered and broke. Her sweat had soaked her hair and the entire back of her dress. She looked down at their entwined hands. Martin's right hand moved in hers. She felt the skin beneath her fingertips. She removed her hands. Martin's, beneath it, was pale and firm and healthy.

She blinked. She closed her eyes and looked again. Martin's hand was still there. Whole.

She looked at Martin and he was grinning, unbelieving, ecstatic.

He flexed his hand. "Sylvie," he said. "Sylvie, it's just fine. You did it! You—"

She got up steadily. She was glad for Martin. Vaguely, she knew that. She pushed her way past the staring, muttering men, past Arnaud, past the cook. She recognized Robert Chouinard's voice saying her name, she saw the bulk of his body before her, and she waited without looking at him for him to move out of her way, which he eventually did. Then she walked past. Tomorrow, she would face

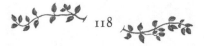

them all, and what they would say, and what they thought.

Witch?

Tomorrow would be soon enough to understand what she had just done.

Tomorrow would be soon enough to question exactly what she was.

CHAPTER

Thirteen

Sylvie was awakened by a rattling jolt as the wagon beneath her descended into a particularly deep rut. Her entire body parted company with the wagon bed, and then she was thrown back down against the saving depth of a tapestry roll. She grasped the side of the wagon and pulled herself to sitting, aware of terror but for a moment not able to recall why she was afraid. Then the sight of her own hand, whole in the early morning sun, reminded her. She looked around hastily for Martin, but she was alone in the wagon.

What she had done for Martin was something new. Something *else* new. Something else to learn to control, to use wisely and well. That thought alone was terrifying. But worse than that was the knowledge that she had done what she had done in *public*, before strangers.

Grand-mère Sylvie had warned her. "There are those who will not believe your gift is from God. That is a separate danger, and it will be all your life, as it is for me."

She'd had no choice but to try to heal Martin, but that did not affect her terror now.

To *lay hands*, Ceciline had called it, speaking of Grand-mère Sylvie. But Grand-mère Sylvie had never been able to heal as dramatically as Sylvie had just done.

And even if she had, Sylvie was alone. She had no grandmother, no mother, to advise her. No Ceciline, either, and not even a woman friend. She thought briefly of the landlady of the inn—who would surely see Sylvie dead for a witch, did she but know of this. Sylvie thought of Father Guillaume, back home. He had known her from a babe, after all. Even Grand-mère Sylvie had called him a friend. What would he think?

Sylvie was praying when the wagon heaved up

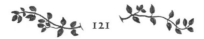

and down into another rut. Her stomach heaved in response. She leaned over the side of the wagon and was helplessly sick, though there was little to come up.

Martin came to her then, climbing up into the wagon, kneeling beside her, patting her back, giving her a rag to wipe her mouth.

"Thank you," Sylvie whispered. "You're all right?" she asked.

For answer he held out his right hand. "I showed you already." Frustration grated in his voice. "Yesterday, and the day before too."

"Oh yes," she said. "Good."

"Robbers tried to attack us last night, in the dark."

"Really?"

"Yes. We formed a ring of defense and killed them all. Well. Or killed many. Or they ran away, once they saw we would not be easy prey. You slept through the whole thing." Martin's tone was reproachful, then eager. "Listen, Sylvie, I got one of them with my slingshot. I'm almost sure of it!"

Sylvie squinted at Martin. "You have a slingshot?"

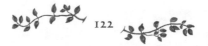

"I made one, remember?" Martin said patiently. "Because Arnaud said we were approaching the place where sometimes the robbers wait. It was very exciting." He waited.

"Oh," said Sylvie. "Yes. No doubt." She paused. "You made a slingshot?"

Martin sighed. "Go back to sleep, Sylvie."

He went away.

Robbers, Sylvie thought. Martin fighting with a slingshot, in danger. She knew she ought to have an opinion about this, or a thought, or an emotion. Instead of finding it, she laid herself down again and closed her eyes, trying to ignore the sickening movement of the wagon. She reached for Grandmère Sylvie's shawl and pulled it around her.

When the sun was much higher in the sky, Martin came back.

"Sylvie, are you ill? It's been two whole days you've been like this."

"I just have to sleep some more," Sylvie said. "Then I will be fine." She told Martin that her grandmother had used to need sleep too, after healing, and that seemed to settle him down.

"I'll sit with you," he decided.

123

Sylvie nodded and smiled and slept.

Sometime later the wagon slammed into another rut. Sylvie opened her eyes, finding herself alone again. She stared up at the cloudless spring sky. Around her, beyond the high sides of the wagon, came the noises of the caravan and the horses and the men. Her head felt clearer now. She wondered if any of the men were looking in her direction. She wondered what they were thinking. She wondered if they would fear her. If they would want to hurt her. If any of them knew priests, inquisitors. This was not Bresnois.

She sat up firmly and looked out. Out and around.

Yes, some eyes met hers and slid away uneasily. Not many; people were busy. The caravan was after all about its own traveling business, and they were now not far from Lyon, where they would move onto barges to take the cargo downriver. But there were some who looked at her oddly, she thought. Yes—there. Yves, staring and paling slightly. Was that the sign of the cross he made, rapidly, discreetly, as he turned away? Stomach clenching again, Sylvie dropped her gaze. From the corner of

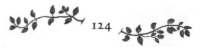

her eye she saw Yves canter back toward the end of the caravan train.

But as she watched Yves, defiance filled her. She was the daughter of Jeanne. The granddaughter of Sylvie. The great-granddaughter of Marthe. Healers all. Strong women all. Even if she was not quite like them, she would hold up her head like them.

But that was the crux, wasn't it? What was she? For she was *not* like the women of her family. Not quite. Jeanne was a healer. Grand-mère Sylvie had been something more: a wisewoman, like Ceciline, with a gift. Marthe . . . who knew? The stories about Marthe had been perfectly ordinary: there was a receipt for an herb tisane that had been hers, a healing potion for insect bites, a brew to brighten hair color. She had been like Jeanne, perhaps. While she, Sylvie, was . . . something else entirely. Something that had alarmed even Grand-mère Sylvie. Something that— she must be honest—something that frightened Sylvie herself.

That was the truth.

She looked at it now, hard and straight, until she understood what had frightened her, and what

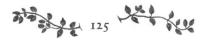

she had been running from ever since she had taken Jeanne's grief from her. She had not been running toward help—as she had thought—and not even from what she had done. She had been running, instead, from herself. From what was inside her, waiting to be found.

Power, Arnaud had said the other night, as he spoke of the de' Medicis. Power. It was what Arnaud admired. What the egg-boy envied. What Robert Chouinard had and doubtless wanted more of. You could be born to power, like a king. You could work your way to earning it. You could buy it, if you had money. You could even steal it, by doing things that made people afraid of you.

She, Sylvie, had power, Sylvie thought. She was not a de' Medici, not a king, not wealthy, not a man. She did not want to hurt anyone. Nevertheless, she had power of a rare kind, she had been given it, and now everyone in this caravan knew it.

One thing was certain, however. She could not hide anymore in Grand-mère Sylvie's shawl. Slowly, she took it off, folded it, and set it aside. Then she lifted her chin and climbed out of the wagon. The rest of the day, she would walk. And she would

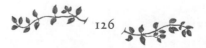

stare everyone she met in the eye, until they—not she—looked away.

And she would do as Jeanne had taught her. She would pray.

Because even if some would not believe it, she was no heretic. No witch.

She was simply Sylvie, a healer.

"You are awake, then." It was Robert Chouinard, speaking with careful courtesy. He had brought his horse beside Sylvie as she walked. She had somehow known that he would come as soon as he saw that she was up. He could be genuinely concerned. But he was also a man who cared about power. She had not known him long, but she knew that. It screamed from him. Ceciline had seemed to trust him, but then, Ceciline had not fully understood about Sylvie.

"You are well?" he asked.

"Yes," said Sylvie.

He dismounted and moved to walk beside her, holding his horse on a rein. For practice, she gave him a straight look. He met it. They walked together. People watched them, as she had known they would. Eventually he began speaking of the journey.

"We'll arrive in Lyon tomorrow. I only plan on two days there; we need to get our cargo to Marseille speedily. There will be barges ready for us, and men to load them."

"Will you have time to take us to the house of Ceciline's friend Madame du Bois?" asked Sylvie. "If not, I am sure we can find it ourselves."

Monsieur Chouinard said slowly, "I'll take you, if you're sure that you really should go—" He stopped. "I'll take you," he finally repeated.

"Thank you. You are very kind."

"No," said his voice beside her. "Kind I am not. I cannot—afford kindness."

Sylvie slanted him a curious look. Robert Chouinard held out his arm. Hesitantly, she took it. His horse ambled obediently behind them. He said, "The woman you are to visit in Lyon, Madame du Bois. Do you know anything of her?"

"No. Do you?"

He seemed to choose his words even more carefully now. "Yes. She's a judicial astrologer, famed for her nativity maps."

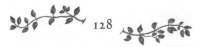

128

Sylvie blinked with surprise and a sharp pang of disappointment, followed by doubt. She had assumed this woman would be a healer, like herself. Or a wisewoman, like Ceciline. How could an astrologer help her? What had Ceciline had in mind? Sylvie didn't even know . . .

"Nativity maps? What are they?" she asked.

His lips twisted in a rueful smile. "A nativity map shows the sky at the moment of your birth, charting the exact positions of the stars, the moon, and the planets as they circle the earth. Supposedly the map determines your prospects in life. Many people, important people, feel it's wise to consult their maps—with the interpretive aid of a good astrologer, of course, such as Madame du Bois—before making any serious decision. Such as marriage, for example." An emotion passed over his face, but Sylvie could not read it.

"Do *you* have such a map?" she asked.

"No. It would be impossible to cast one for me, since I am not sure when I was born, or of"—his hesitation lasted only a moment—"or of my parentage. In any event, I am a gambler by nature. And not the type of client Madame du Bois would want.

I understand she sees bankers and merchants and lords. Even a prince, once." Another careful pause, longer this time. "Her client list—so I hear—also includes some very high churchmen. A cardinal. At least one archbishop. Even if they have had maps cast for them before, many want hers instead; her skill is that well regarded."

Churchmen. *High* churchmen—unlike Father Guillaume.

Sylvie said nothing.

Robert Chouinard pursued: "Now, I ask myself, why would Ceciline send you to see someone like that?"

She snapped: "What are you trying to say, Monsieur?"

He didn't answer. Instead, he said: "Why did you leave your home?"

"That's not your business."

He did not take offense, as far as she could tell. His eyes weighed and measured. Then he seemed to come to some decision. "Sylvie. I would like to speak with you in private." He indicated the caravan around them, the covert eyes. "This is hardly that. A short ride? I could take you up before me."

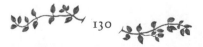

She had never been on a grand, tall horse before.

Without turning, she knew Martin was near, his among the eyes on them. What would he think of this?

Robert Chouinard was waiting easily for her answer. Had he ever called her by her name before? She did not think so.

She was curious. He had been talking around *something* for this entire conversation. "Very well," Sylvie said with composure, and let him toss her up on the horse.

Fourteen

Behind them the noise of the caravan's travel faded. They went some way without speaking. Sylvie had never before been on a mount higher than a donkey, and she concentrated on becoming accustomed to the motion coupled with the height from the ground. Robert Chouinard held her securely; she did not fear falling. His arm at her waist was warm and polite and well muscled. She felt very aware of its strength.

She felt aware of *him*, more than ever, and not just physically.

The truth was that she had been curious about

Robert since the market in Montigny. Given what the egg-boy had said about Robert's past, and also his mysterious connection with Ceciline, he was not the spoiled and arrogant person she had at first assumed. But what he actually was—*who* he was at the level of his character—that was unknown. She had all this while been sorely tempted to study him and learn more, but had tamped down her interest. In part, because she knew Martin would not like it.

And in other part, because she had not wanted to admit her interest to herself.

Now she admitted it. He *did* interest her. Robert was young, yet he was the master of the caravan. He was the one the others called "he" without needing to specify whom they meant. In the caravan, what Robert thought, what he might *do*, about her, about Martin—all of it mattered now. There was no Ceciline to intervene. No anyone. Yes, even if he were not interesting in and of himself, it was now personally important to Sylvie to understand Robert better. She ought also to be anxious—and, perhaps, afraid of him, she realized. But now, alone with him, she discovered that she was not. Her feeling of calm remained.

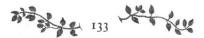 133

They reached a small wood. Robert dismounted and helped her down. Ahead was a stream.

Near it, Sylvie noted Solomon's seal, thriving in the damp. Jeanne would have taken some for help in healing wounds; Sylvie's fingers itched to do the same, but now was not the time to gather supplies. Out of habit, she continued scanning the ground: there, just edging its leaves up, was blue flag. In a few weeks, it would flower into stunning violet-and-gold beauty. Its roots, taken internally, were poison.

Monsieur Chouinard indicated a large, flat-topped rock by the stream. "Would you like to sit?" he asked.

Sylvie shook her head. She turned to face him and had to look up. It crimped her nape.

He was regarding her gravely. She said, "However, *you* can sit if you like."

He gave up the advantage of height with ease. He leaned his elbows on his knees and looked up at her as if she were as much a curiosity to him, as he to her. He said, "You are seventeen, Sylvie? Or perhaps eighteen?" He used her name casually, as if he owned it.

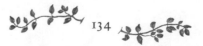 134

She said composedly, "I shall not be sixteen until next year."

"Fifteen." The barest flicker of dismay crossed his expression; had she not been watching so closely, she would have missed it. "Ah. Not any longer a child, and yet . . ." He was silent for so long that Sylvie almost spoke unwarily, anything to break the quiet. But then he added evenly, as if it were inconsequential: "I need to tell you. There is an inquisitor in Lyon."

After the days of sickness and sleep, and the fear she had felt whenever she wakened, and indeed, perhaps even while she slept, she found it was a relief to have this discussion openly. "An inquisitor?" Blessedly, her voice was as even as his.

"Yes. With a bull from the pope to question suspected heretics, including witches. I have met him, and he seems to me rather a strange man. So if you were to stay in Lyon as you intend, with Madame du Bois, you could be in some danger." He added after a moment: "You've been imprudent on this journey. People *will* talk."

A bit tartly, she said, "Prudence did not enter into it. Martin needed help."

 135

Robert nodded grimly. "I understand that. I meant no blame."

He leaned forward, gaze intent—and then words burst forth from him as never before, frankly, all formality cast aside. "Sylvie. Could you go home if you wished? Or is there someone there who would hurt you? Another inquisitor, or a priest? Is that why you left?"

Only for a moment was it shocking that Robert Chouinard spoke to her as if to one he knew well. But then Sylvie found herself answering with the same simplicity. "In Bresnois? No." She thought of happy, overeducated Father Guillaume. Of how his face always lit up when she and Jeanne visited him. "I should not teach females, perhaps," he had chided himself aloud once. "But when they are the ones who wish to learn, why not? Mary sat at the feet of our Lord to learn. So, Sylvie, here is a Latin verse for you to translate into French. Mind the irregular verb *esse*; we shall conjugate it together. Jeanne, when Sylvie finishes, as a treat, you shall recite for us the eight Beatitudes of Matthew." It was a good memory and a calming one.

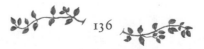

Sylvie added now, to Robert, who was listening intently: "I could go home and be safe there. I *want* to go home. Only I can't. For other reasons. I shall one day, but I cannot go there yet."

"Even if you would," he said, frowning, "I confess that I cannot think how you would get there. I've spent two days now thinking about it. I would take you, but I must get to Marseille first. I'd trust Arnaud to take you, but I need him with me. In a couple of months, it will be different."

She was stunned. He had been thinking and thinking about how to assist her? How to keep her safe?

"Thank you," she said at last. "For thinking of me." She hesitated. She opened her mouth and impulsively added: "What do you think of—of what I did? Do you think I am a witch?"

His face told her nothing at first. He said merely: "Does it matter to you what I think?"

Did it *matter*? She was speechless.

He pushed one hand up into his hair. He said: "Very well. I like you, Sylvie. And—witch or no—I feel you are nothing to fear." Oddly, then he looked away, looked down, almost as if he were shy. "I

 137

think—I think you should be protected, prized. Cared for. Not hunted. Not feared."

Not feared?

He was wrong.

Sylvie made a sudden decision: to tell him the truth. She said: "Listen to me, Monsieur." She deliberately chose to be more formal, not to use his given name. "I *am* dangerous. I am a healer, this I know, but it is all I know. I wish to use my gift for good. But think of me as belike an apprentice who has no master. I have inherited tools but I have no experience and little knowledge. What happened with Martin—that was new. I do not know what I can do. I need to learn, or I will make mistakes. *That* is the danger. That is why I sought Ceciline, or one like her. That is why I need to speak to this Madame du Bois, whom Ceciline feels might help me. That is why I am traveling."

She looked levelly at him.

The stream babbled.

After a moment, Robert nodded his understanding. Then he was quiet, considering what she had said. At last he spoke: "And you trust Ceciline to guide this new power of yours?"

He did not. That was abundantly clear from his tone. And that was news. Sylvie said slowly: "She was my grandmother's friend. And she's a healer, like me." She raised a wry eyebrow and tried a smile. "To be honest, it does not seem to me that I have a vast choice in teachers. I must make do with what I find."

"She is *not* like you," Robert said slowly. "This I know." He paused, seemingly choosing his words even more carefully. "I have known Ceciline for many years. I owe her my life and she has been a good friend to me. In a way. But I must warn you that she only does things that will benefit her. If I were you, I would not trust her fully. Or—those she recommends."

"*You* are one she recommends," Sylvie pointed out. She did not say *And I have chosen just now to trust you*, for it was obvious.

He nodded. "And it would be wise for you to be wary of me as well. Indeed, you should be wary of everyone."

"It is no way to live," observed Sylvie.

"Is it not?" said Robert Chouinard sharply.

They looked at each other. Sylvie was the first

to look away. For all that he had phrased his opinion as a question and she had not, it was plain that Robert was more certain of his position than she was, at this moment, of hers.

If she was honest with herself.

Sylvie said, "Very well. I'll be careful with Madame du Bois, and also with Ceciline, if I should see her again."

"Oh, you will see her again."

There were a few moments of utter quiet. Then Robert said: "If you will not go home, I have had another idea. It would, I think, work. You could marry me."

From his face, he might have just said that the weather would turn.

He went on, unhurriedly but with some return of formality. "It would afford you some protection. Very likely it would be enough. People—my men, especially—would be more reluctant to make accusations against you if they knew they would have to face me as well."

Sylvie's mind reeled. She could not imagine his motives. She said carefully: "It is a drastic solution. And dangerous for you, surely."

He shook his head. "On balance, I don't think so. My men are loyal to me—or at least to what working with me offers them—and I believe I have enough standing to weather a small storm. We could marry as soon as we arrive in Lyon. And though I must go on to Marseille, you would still have my protection while you visit Madame du Bois. That might be useful if she has her tame bishops in. And the marriage needn't be permanent. We could get an annulment later." He smiled, but there was no amusement in it. "And if Ceciline is up to something—she won't have anticipated this turn of events."

His brain skipped around like a goat on wine, assessing this, calculating that. Sylvie could follow him, however, and even notice something he either hadn't, or didn't want to mention, or simply hoped she wouldn't see. He expected her to trust him, but he, as he had said, trusted nobody and nothing, including his supposed friend Ceciline.

She said, "Aren't you overreacting? No one has turned me in for a witch yet. Maybe no one will."

His mouth twisted in patent disbelief—even amusement?—at her naivete.

It infuriated her. "If you are so determined to protect me, and you're important enough to do it—well, can't you help without marrying me? Use your influence . . . or something?"

He said evenly: "I suppose I could. That might work. Or better, bribes."

She caught her breath.

"But then again, it might not. First, understand that there will be talk about you. It's too good a story, what you have done to heal Martin's hand. It will be told. There will be rumors and whispers. And I will not be there in person. I can stay in Lyon only for two days, as long as it takes to load our cargo on barges."

"But unless someone actually tells a priest, or this inquisitor—"

"Someone will. Do you think I don't know my own men?"

Sylvie thought again of Yves. "But can't you—?"

"What? Forbid them to talk?" His voice was quite level. He added, incredibly: "Or would you like me to kill the ones most likely to speak? Who's your top candidate for death? Yves, my accountant and sometime aide-de-camp? Ah, I see we are in

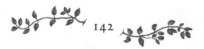

agreement there. I would be sad. It isn't as easy as you might think to find someone who knows Italian double-entry bookkeeping."

Was that a smile?

She was appalled.

He was looking past her now, his face analytical again. He said: "It would probably work, killing Yves. For a while. We could start with killing just the one man. It'll scare the others into keeping their mouths shut. Maybe." He arced an eyebrow. "Yves must die, then? I must say, I don't think much of it as a long-term solution. Plus, I'd really thought my days of murder and mayhem were over. Enjoyable though they were, at times."

Was he joking? She couldn't tell. His mind was as twisty as a bramble bush. Sylvie said stiffly: "Stop making fun of me. This is serious."

"You are the one who seems not to understand that."

He turned everything around. She said, "What I don't understand is why you think marriage to you is the only solution."

"Not the only solution, as I have said. Merely the most certain to work. Possibly the most moral.

And—let me be frank—the most convenient for me."

"Convenient?"

He said patiently, "This is a business trip. I am twenty-four, which is young for my position and I am still building—I need this trip. I need to get my cargo and myself to Marseille. I have time for a quick wedding in Lyon. I do *not* have time to see if any of my men place witchcraft allegations against you. I do not have time to wait on your business with Madame du Bois. I do not have time to worry about how Ceciline might be planning to use you. I do not have time for confidential discussions with officials about whether you are or are not a witch, or for calculating whom to bribe and how much to bribe them. Certainly I do not have time to bear witness at a witchcraft trial, prolonged or otherwise. Do you understand me now?"

Color climbed on her cheeks. "Yes."

"Good," he said. He got up. "It's settled, then. We shall marry."

"No," said Sylvie. "We shall not."

He looked at her. Looked down at her for what felt like a very long time. Then he said: "It's your

144

right to take a risk with yourself, of course. But what about Martin? You don't look like sister and brother, you and Martin. Not that it matters; brother or no, I don't care. But you have made him unsafe now, as well as yourself."

"No," said Sylvie. "Surely I have not."

"Yes. Listen to me. Martin could be hurt by those who think him your brother. Or think him bewitched." He added bluntly: "How would you feel if Martin were killed because of you? He will defend you, or try. You know this."

He said more. He said quite a lot, all of it logical. She heard it all. Finally he stopped.

She had fixed her eyes beyond him, on the blue flag. She said quietly: "Martin must be safe."

"If you marry me," said Monsieur Chouinard, "Martin will be protected too. And I assure you, you need not be frightened of me. You can trust me. It is only a temporary solution. We will get an annulment later."

"Be entirely clear with me," Sylvie said with a flash of anger. "You mean you do not intend to bed me? Will you promise me this, and an annulment upon my request?" She thought, but did not say,

of all else that he was asking her to trust him with, for it was far more than her body. Once married, he would own her. He could do anything he liked with her, and the world would call it his right. He had power and wanted more of it; he might even be angling to control her gift.

A flush rose on his face. "Yes, that is what I mean, and yes, of course I promise you. It is not unusual, in any case, for a man to wait for a very young bride to mature before risking her in child-birth. No one would say anything if they were to know we did not share a bed. Our marriage would still be considered valid. But then, later, it would be easy to annul. Why do you roll your eyes?"

"Because," said Sylvie. "I was thinking of the king of England, with his case before the pope."

"He will never get an annulment," said Robert positively. "But that is nothing to do with our situation."

Sylvie nodded. She took a deep breath. "I thank you. I believe what you say. But I don't wish to marry, not you or anyone. Not even temporarily. And I see no need. No one has yet reported me to

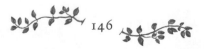

this inquisitor. And I am innocent. I am no heretic, no witch. I am a good Christian."

Robert's eyes were like stones. He said, "I understand that you don't *wish* to marry me. And I also understand that I am not—not every young maiden's dream of a good husband. But I am asking if you *will*. Given our—unusual—circumstances."

Sylvie bit her lip.

She might be wise to say yes. She found that she believed Robert could protect her. She also believed he was right about his men. Someone would talk. Yves, or another.

But men *owned* their wives. And while she wanted to understand Robert, who he was, what he was made of, she did not know him at this time. She did not.

He was the one who had warned her not to trust anyone.

"No," she said at last. "I will not marry you. I will take care of myself, and I will take care of Martin. But still, Robert." Now she used his name. "I thank you for your kind offer."

"You are a fool." Robert said it impassively.

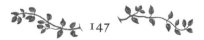

"I am not a fool," Sylvie said steadily. "You don't know me."

"And you don't know the world."

"Nonetheless, I will take care of myself."

He snorted.

"Did you always know the world?" Sylvie demanded. "You survived, did you not?"

"At cost—" He snapped his mouth shut. He walked a few steps away and stood there for a few minutes. She watched his back.

She wondered what the cost had been.

Eventually he turned to her. His face was impassive. He said, "I have your answer, then. Now we must return." He caught his horse and cupped his hands for her to mount. She did, and he climbed up behind her and held her.

If anything, she was more aware than before of the strength of his arms around her as they traveled.

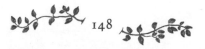

CHAPTER
Fifteen

On the ride back, Sylvie tried not to think about how good, how safe, it felt simply to be in Robert's arms. She had much to turn over in her mind. She would have been grateful for the distraction of her thoughts, if those thoughts had not been so disturbing and yet so necessary.

Every instinct told her she could not agree to Robert's—she found that she could no longer think of him as Monsieur—proposal. Of course she did not want to pay the steep price of marriage: to mortgage her future, to place it in his hands, to abdicate her own responsibility for herself and Martin. To a man who distrusted everyone, besides, and whom she did not know well? It was too much of a blind leap.

Beyond that, however, she questioned whether Robert could truly protect her and Martin, or if he only hoped he could. His confidence in this matter had been persuasive, but he was twenty-four, he had said, and still building his life. This was more than eight years older than she, but surely not enough to have true power, not when you came from nothing. Sylvie well remembered the egg-boy's ugly comments. Robert had enemies and ill will; he had no family at his back. If he were to marry her and she were accused of witchcraft, it might destroy him. Had he thought of that? Foolish question; one thing she knew was that he did not lack for calculating, assessing intelligence. He had thought of it. Which meant . . . which meant he had decided to take a risk. For her sake.

Sylvie's throat caught with feelings that she dared not examine too closely. One was that he was, perhaps after all, a fool. The other—

Oh, this she knew: she had done right in refusing.

Sylvie had come from a family of women who managed, if sometimes only precariously, to remain in charge of their own lives. "Even the best men desire to control their women," Grand-mère Sylvie had said once, pragmatically, to Jeanne, who agreed: "Even when their motives are good, the box can grow very tight." The two women had not been looking at Sylvie, then only twelve, as they talked. But she had known their words were meant for her to hear. Hear and consider, when it was time to make her own choices.

Now Sylvie—her stomach clenching—thought that Robert's plan was noble, but, though he could not know it, unnecessary. She herself could stop Yves—stop all of the men of the caravan, if need be—from endangering herself or Martin.

She could use the part of her gift about which Robert knew nothing.

Was it wicked, a misuse of her power? She did not know, and there was no Grand-mère Sylvie to ask. But this she did know: the other choice, to depend on Robert, was not acceptable or fair to herself, to Martin, or to Robert himself.

And so, Sylvie began to plan.

When they reached the caravan and Robert helped her to alight, she did not have far to go to find Martin. He had left Arnaud and—uncharacteristically—was sitting cross-legged in the wagon's bed, body jostling as the wheels descended into and lurched out of every rut on the road. He was scowling, and his eyes accused her as she climbed in and sat facing him.

Words burst from him. "Where did you go with him? What did he say to you? Why did he have his arm around you?"

Sylvie answered the last question first, levelly. "To keep me on the horse."

"No, that's not why. I've seen him notice you. From the first time we met him, I've seen him look, and now—"

Martin was not imagining things, Sylvie was forced to acknowledge. A man did not think to propose marriage when any unmarried woman near him seemed to need protection. Oh, it did not matter now, with Martin on the brink of rage. She put her hand over his mouth briefly, gently. As if she had done it before, she used the mildest of mind

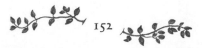

touches to reach and soothe him. He calmed; she felt it. She said, "Listen to me, Martin. Please. I need your help."

He nodded.

She contained her wonderment at what she had just done—and her worry. Was it so easy to slip into using her power—and was it misuse?

She told Martin about the inquisitor in Lyon and, so that he would understand fully how serious this was, started to tell him about a witchcraft trial that Grand-mère Sylvie had faced thirty-five years before. She had been imprisoned rather than killed—a reprieve intended to be temporary—because she had been pregnant with Jeanne. It was a well-known story in Sylvie's family.

Incredibly, however, Martin already knew the story. He nodded. "She escaped the prison," he said. "After your mother was born. They thought her too weak from the birth to run, but they were wrong. And Ceciline helped her after that. She hid your grandmother and the baby until it was safe for them to leave that city."

Sylvie stared, surprised. Ceciline had been

involved? Her understanding was that Grand-mère Sylvie had imposed her will on the prison guard, and he let her slip away. Then someone had hidden her—oh.

"The person who hid her," she said to Martin. "You say it was Ceciline?"

He nodded. "While you slept that night, Ceciline asked me how well I knew your grandmother. I told her how often we talked. When I said I knew about Grand-mère Sylvie escaping prison, she explained that she was the friend in the story."

"Oh," said Sylvie, frowning.

"What is it?"

"Nothing," said Sylvie. "It's just that I never heard tell of Ceciline before we went to Montigny. I wonder, why didn't Grand-mère Sylvie mention her by name? Why did we have no contact with her? Montigny is not *that* far."

"Ceciline said they decided, after your grandmother escaped, that it was safer for the both of them to part forever. And she was afraid herself, since she did not want to be accused of witchcraft too."

That made sense, Sylvie supposed.

Yes, it fit.

At least one thing was clear now: Robert had been wrong about Ceciline—his carefully worded distrust of her was wrong. At great risk, Ceciline had helped Grand-mère Sylvie all those years ago.

Perhaps, just perhaps, he was wrong about other things as well? Was there any danger at all for Sylvie?

Just then, however, she saw Yves on his horse ten yards away, and even from there she could see what was in his eyes.

Robert had not been wrong, and she should not waste her time in hope.

She reached for her pack and her small store of supplies, which Jeanne had trained her to have always with her, and told Martin her plan.

She would need his help.

✑

In some ways Martin's part was riskiest. He'd long since befriended the cook, but never before had volunteered to help him cook dinner. But the cook seemed unsuspicious. He, at least, was not among those who would wish to harm Martin.

Sylvie waited until Martin was positioned by

the fire, stirring the potage. Then she stepped forward and called his name, advancing a few steps. As she spoke, the cook's eyes were drawn away from Martin and to her.

And there, Sylvie saw the wariness, the suspicion. It stiffened her spine. "Are you sure that work's not too hot for you, Martin?" she said, and then added deliberately: "I mean, for your right hand? The skin may still be very new and sensitive."

In the instant in which she first spoke, while the cook's attention was momentarily on Sylvie, Martin acted. Single-handed, deft, he drew Sylvie's small flask of belladonna from his pocket, withdrew the cork with two fingers, and dumped its contents into the pot. He was done, palming the flask, as the cook turned back to hear his answer, his gaze inevitably on not Martin's left hand, but his right, innocently stirring the pot.

"My hand is fine," said Martin smoothly. "It feels the same as ever."

Sylvie nodded. "Be careful with it," she said, and in those two seconds Martin pocketed the empty flask. Sylvie withdrew, feeling not relieved but

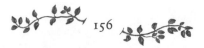

frightened. The first part was done and could not be undone. And it was her responsibility.

Belladonna. Fair lady. Dwale. Deadly night-shade. It was at once a lethal poison and a valuable remedy—too valuable for a healer to ever be without. It was from Jeanne that Sylvie had learned to find the berries when they ripened in early autumn, to crush them for their juice, and to save the juice against future need. It was from Jeanne that Sylvie had learned the power of belladonna against ailments of the stomach, and of its side effect: sleepiness.

Or, if the quantity was overcalculated, its other side effect: a deep unnatural sleep, followed by death.

There was little room for error; the tiniest miscalculation could be fatal. And Sylvie had only learned the dosage for a single person. It had made sense to multiply the amount by eighteen, for the twenty members of the caravan—minus Martin and herself—that would drink it.

But plant lore did not always make mathematical sense, and, moreover, would the belladonna

 157

dilute properly in the potage? Would everyone eat their share? What about second or third helpings, what about differently sized appetites, what about differently sized men? There were so many variables that her head had ached trying to think of them all. Trying to determine if she had adjusted for as many as she could. In fact she could not be sure. She was lucky that she'd had sufficient belladonna with her at all.

She hadn't burdened Martin with her doubts about the dosage. Feigning total confidence, she had told him only that the belladonna would cause everyone to sleep heavily. She needed Martin's help, but if things went wrong, she alone should bear the moral responsibility. She should not involve Martin more than she needed to.

That was her mistake.

She only realized it when it was too late. For as the members of the caravan party took their potage—including Robert, who was no different from anyone else to her, he was not—Martin joined them. Under her horrified eye, with full confidence in her, and against every assumption she had made, Martin helped himself to a huge portion. Took it

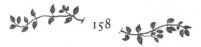

and ate it, grinning at her—thus turning her eighteen into nineteen. And in so doing, he changed the risk of death for the men into a different risk: the risk that one or more of them, insufficiently dosed, would awaken. Would awaken when Sylvie most desperately needed them to sleep.

"They would have noticed if I hadn't eaten too," Martin said cheerfully fifteen minutes later, when Sylvie—disciplining herself to reveal nothing but inquiry, for there was no sense now in alarming him—asked. He yawned. "It was all right for you to eat only bread—they think you're strange anyway—but they'd have been suspicious of me, and maybe remembered later. I always eat everything I can."

"Yes," Sylvie managed to say. She wondered frantically, should she try to force him to throw up? Only Martin was already swaying on his feet, and the men were nearby and awake.

She watched him almost stumble toward their wagon. One large bowl, and he was so small. He would sleep. Surely Martin would simply sleep.

All she could do now was wait for *everyone* to sleep, and pray they did so soundly—even those

who were usually on watch. And that she would be able to use her gift on Yves while he was unconscious—she had never so much as looked into a sleeping mind. And that tonight they would be undisturbed by robbers, or worse.

And—and—and.

And suddenly she thought: Perhaps Grand-mère Sylvie and Jeanne were not entirely correct when they discussed how women were forced to give up power and control of their own lives. Perhaps sometimes they *chose*. Perhaps giving up power and control—giving up responsibility—was something that many people, male and female both, would positively desire.

Then you would not have to bear the weight of your own actions when, through erroneous planning or pure happenstance, they went all wrong.

Where is my teacher? Sylvie thought miserably. Where is she? I need her. I *need* her.

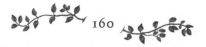

She lay by Martin, waiting, and listening to him breathe. To her relief his breathing seemed heavy, slow, but steady. He would be fine, she thought. She chose not to think of the implications for the men's dosages, Robert's included. Not now. It was, after all, too late for that.

The camp was quiet. Time passed: minutes, an hour. When the moon rose, so did Sylvie.

She moved noiselessly away from the wagon. Her pulse pounded in her throat.

Most of the men slept roughly on the ground in the open, with a few in small tents, and a couple of wagon drivers with their cargo. Sylvie visited them all briefly, touching their temples, querying, and finding no malign intentions toward herself or Martin. Hoping against hope that this would be good enough, she left them alone.

She hesitated an extra moment or two near Robert, tempted to search his mind—find out more about why he'd suggested marrying her—find out what he'd meant about the cost he'd paid for being in the world. But no. No, this was not her priority, and also it was wrong, and also there might not be enough time.

She went to Yves.

He slept near three other men, a bulky lump beneath a blanket, his head pillowed on one arm. She knelt by him, inches away, hearing the faint

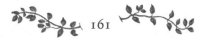

whistling noise of impeded nostrils and slightly clogged lungs. He had a cold. If he had asked, she would have brewed him hyssop tea.

Instead—if she could—she would steal his thoughts.

She placed her fingertips gently on his forehead. She reached with her own mind and fished delicately around in his, searching. Looking for herself.

She saw shades of women, less individuals than a race, unknown, vaguely disdained, not important. Even with her encouragement, he would not dwell on any of them. Money, now that was important to him, and power. The money dreams danced prominently at the front of Yves's mind, forcing themselves on her, displaying themselves. Fantasies—silly—he would amaze them all with his shrewdness, his success. He would amaze someone in particular: strong and clear as water, Sylvie could see an older man's face, full of imagined pride and love. Yves's father. Oh, Yves loved his father, wanted his love and respect, though the man was now with God. Sylvie winced away, ashamed. She had no business there.

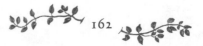

She sifted further, faster, more randomly, amazed that she could do this but having no time to dwell on it. There was so much there. How could she make sense of this mess? There was no organization, no key, no map. And the images, the thoughts, more and more and more of them, pouring in.

It was overwhelming, and she began to panic. Yves stirred, feeling her distress, sharing it, and at the last moment she pulled her hand away. He shifted slightly, murmured something, but did not wake. She was lucky, she thought.

She sat back on her heels. She had not expected this. This was not like touching the thing at the very front of a person's conscious mind and reading it. She had no idea how to find the thoughts she wanted. And if she could not find them, she could not remove them.

Where was her teacher?

Nowhere. She was alone. She forced herself to calm, to concentrate. She just needed a way in, surely. A key. Something besides herself to hunt for in the chaos of Yves's head. Something strong enough to get his attention and focus it. Something

that would *lead* to her. Something powerful that was associated with her.

When she finally lit upon it, it was simple. Robert. Of course.

She pictured Robert in her own mind. The height. The shoulders. The stone eyes and the mind like rootstock. She replaced her hand on Yves's temple, gently, and transferred the image to him.

And was rewarded with a rush of emotions, pictures, thoughts. They were not unlike the fantasies she'd seen earlier in Yves's mind. In fact, they were strikingly similar, with only one real difference. In the memories, Robert was the focus. In the fantasies, he was replaced by Yves.

She wanted to laugh. Yves's fantasies and dreams were not original. They were near copies of Robert's reality—as Yves perceived it.

But it was not just admiration or the desire to emulate in Yves's mind. There was envy. An impulse to do damage, if he could do so safely and profitably. Not laughable, these.

It was there, among the possible damage that Yves might cause Robert, that she finally found herself in Yves's mind. And yes, the intention to report

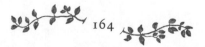

her to the Lyon inquisitor was there. But it was not motivated by fear of witches or dislike or fear of Sylvie. It was about Robert and how Sylvie might be used as a weapon against him.

Martin was not the only one, then, who felt that Robert watched Sylvie with interest—but she would not think about that now. She focused.

The whole morass of Yves's thoughts about Robert seemed to her almost a physical thing. She could take it out. That was what she had done with Jeanne. And she had vowed never to do that again.

But Sylvie had a right to protect herself and Martin, didn't she? What if this were the only way?

Yves was near the surface of sleep, and Sylvie was hesitating. She calmed him with gentle, soothing thoughts. But if he was almost ready to awaken, the other men would be too. She had very little time left. Even Martin might be stirring.

Martin. The thought was like a gift. It gave her yet another possible key. She held her breath and looked for Martin in the tangled mass of Yves's thoughts about Robert. And found him. He occupied very little room in Yves's mind compared to Robert. Compared even to herself. And it was a

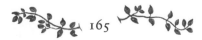

nice, compact, self-contained group of memories and thoughts, one that she could remove easily and, she hoped, with much less damage.

It was the best she could do. She took Yves's most vivid memories of Martin and pulled them out, leaving—she thought, she hoped—only a musty recollection of a boy as one of the travelers. Then she edged away and stood, and saw the first faint pink of the dawn on the eastern horizon.

She should have felt triumphant. But she did not. She felt empty.

Sixteen

"Well?" asked Martin that morning. He rubbed his head. "Did it work? I hope so. I have a headache."

From what Sylvie could see, so did everyone else in their camp. All the men were stumbling about, muttering. "I think so," said Sylvie. "I made him forget anything detailed about you."

"I'd better keep out of his way, then," said Martin.

Sylvie nodded dully. Would someone else notice Yves's new notion of Martin, find it peculiar, suspect witchcraft, suspect her? Would Robert?

Another thing she had not thought of as she fumbled with her gift and the hazards of using it. Was taking action in a crisis always like that?

Yves went about his morning chores. He didn't look worse than anyone else. He was checking on the horses. Eating some bread. Behaving normally. It was done now, and she could no more undo this than she could undo what she had done to Jeanne.

Both times her motives had been good.

No, she thought. This time, her motive had been less good. This time, she had not had ignorance as an excuse.

"No more," she whispered to herself. "I won't do it again." And knew, even as she said it, that she was lying.

Robert had said that Sylvie was nothing to fear. He was wrong, very wrong. He did not know her. But she had been wrong, too—wrong to think that she could rely on herself alone.

She needed a teacher, someone she could trust fully.

And if this Madame du Bois in Lyon could not help her, she did not know what she would do.

168

They arrived in Lyon in late afternoon. Sylvie gasped involuntarily when she first saw it, sitting between the rivers Rhône and Saône. She had expected merely a bigger version of Montigny. A larger town. She had not expected a city. She had not known what a city was.

How could a place be so crammed with buildings and with people? Be so starkly, so unrepentantly, filled with busyness? Paved cobblestone streets. Alehouses, docks, shops, stalls, dwellings to house not one but several families, alleys. The spires of a cathedral. Clerks, ladies, flower sellers, beggars.

Entering Lyon felt like dropping down into a huge well. The sky seemed higher, farther away, unimportant next to the determined pace and rhythm of the city where everything important was man-made.

As she stared, Sylvie wondered: How could anyone know anyone else in this place? All the people and all the buildings looked somehow alike. It was some kind of wariness, of tension, perhaps, in their eyes, in their facades.

The place pulsed.

 169

"Martin." She clutched his hand.

Martin squeezed her hand back, but with excitement, not fear. "Oh, Sylvie. After Paris, it's the biggest city in France. And we're here. Me, I'm here! Arnaud says . . ."

Sylvie listened as Martin parroted Arnaud. Lyon: crossroads of trade, a hub for goods distributed throughout France, the Swiss Confederation, and the German states of the Holy Roman Empire.

Why did they care about these things? So what if silk could go from Foochow in China by boat to Ormuz in Persia, and from thence overland to Trebizond on the Black Sea, and from thence by boat again across the Mediterranean to Marseille and upriver to Lyon? Did silk make people happy, healthy? Did ivory from Ceylon, or perfumes from Arabia? Sugar could be shipped, and wine and spices, but not meat or bread or fruit.

Nothing truly important required to be raced around the world. Did it?

Why didn't people like Martin and Arnaud and Robert see that it would be better to stay at home and grow what you needed, and trade what you had quietly with your near neighbors, and give away

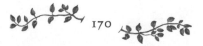

what you did not need yourself? Why did anyone *want* all these exotic things? Why did anyone care what they were, and where they could be found, and how they could be transported, and what they could be purchased and sold for, and how they might invest the proceeds from the first sale, and the second, and the one after that?

Sylvie did not care about any of it. She would go home this very minute if she could. She would be with Jeanne, who knew what was important.

Except that Jeanne did not know her own daughter.

Sylvie felt sudden despair. Her life was gone, gone—and how could anyone who lived here, in this filthy, frightening place, help her?

She said viciously to Martin, "You sound like Robert! Is he your hero now?" and watched Martin's face crumple.

And when he said, "It has nothing to do with Monsieur Chouinard, I just want to see the world, I always wanted . . ." she turned her back on him and would not listen. Because he was from home! He ought to know better! He ought not to want more.

Now she was the one with the headache.

The caravan went through Lyon's central streets directly to the Quai Saint-Antoine on the river Saône. The quay was crowded with warehouses. Boats of all shapes and sizes and states of repair docked in the river. South of Lyon, the Saône merged with the mightier Rhône and then flowed swiftly on to the Mediterranean Sea. Once on the river, a journey that would have taken two weeks by land could be completed in three or four days—while carrying considerably more cargo.

Barges were ready for them, due to Robert's impeccable planning, Sylvie supposed. Extra men were already assembled to begin the loading.

Yves scurried to and fro importantly, even happily, with a vast list. As far as Sylvie could tell, he was fine. At one point, his gaze even moved, indifferently, over Martin and herself. She took a moment to pray a silent thanks to God for that at least. And for the health of all the men. She had seemingly done no real harm.

Luck, she reminded herself. Not skill.

Robert spoke quietly with one after another of the assembled men, his eyes gone cool and

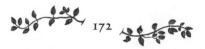

assessing, flickering from their faces to his stock, as the lengthy process of loading started. Sylvie and Martin stood together, not speaking, watching.

Martin was clearly fascinated. Sylvie was not. Her hands were cold, and she knew she was breathing too quickly, but she could not calm herself.

Ceciline's friend Madame du Bois, thought Sylvie. She must go to this Madame du Bois and get her advice—pray God it be quickly given. She did not dare to think what she would do if Madame du Bois wanted her to stay and learn here in Lyon. She would not be easy in her soul, she thought, until she left this hateful, hateful place. It was not just the press of the buildings. She was afraid, afraid for her life, in a way she had never been before. Even now she imagined the prick of eyes at her back. Spying. Suspicious. She thought of the landlady in Montigny turning on her.

She had not expected to feel this way.

She could feel the offended pride radiating off Martin's small body at her side. Directed at her. She had hurt him, but right now she could not care overmuch.

She was too anxious.

 173

Robert was supposed to take her—take them—to this Madame du Bois. Of course that promise was less important than his precious cargo. Sylvie could wait. She was sure that was what he thought. She was forced to wait; she could never find her way alone in this huge maze, this dark, smell-infested, ugly city. She spun on her heel and walked away from Martin.

From her self-imposed distance, she watched Martin shrug defiantly and approach Arnaud. Soon Martin, too, was involved in the loading process, stationed by a winch and shouting when cargo was lifted high enough for transfer, grinning proudly when it landed safely.

Sylvie settled herself out of the way, seated on the ground just outside the entrance to the nearest warehouse. She saw Robert's scanning eyes note her situation in passing, saw him nod as if satisfied, as if she were exactly where he felt she should be. This, too, infuriated her.

Martin, Robert, Yves, Arnaud—they were all busy. It was really the ideal time for her to go and see Madame du Bois. Once she met her, Sylvie felt, she would know instantly if Madame du Bois could

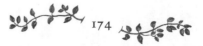

174

or could not help her. Sylvie almost hoped not: then she could get out of here and go—somewhere.

She pulled out the letter and looked, again, at the address. *Madame du Bois. Croix-Rousse. Lyon.* She considered.

If Madame du Bois were as important a lady as Robert had said, the great adviser to great men with her nativity maps, then she would live in a big, important part of town. So this Croix-Rousse must be a big, important place, which people would know about and could direct her to. If she asked them.

If she asked anyone.

It was not sensible to go by herself, but suddenly she could not wait a moment longer. Probably no one here at the quay would even notice that she was gone.

For all that she needed a teacher, she was not helpless on her own—she had proven that.

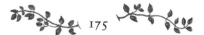

Seventeen

Not far now, Sylvie said to herself as she walked in the growing dusk. Surely not far?

She had gotten directions as easily as she had hoped, and followed the quays north, slipping unremarked through the busy crowds in her rural clothes. Soon, to the right, she should find the rue de l'Annonciade. Yes, there it was.

In her pocket, against the skin of her palm, she felt Ceciline's letter to Madame du Bois. She touched it gently, rubbing the fabric of the paper with her fingertips. She imagined what Madame du Bois would be like. Powerful in mysterious ways, like Grand-mère Sylvie, like Ceciline. And knowledgeable, caring, open-hearted, like Jeanne.

She stopped again for directions. The first person she asked did not know. The second stared at her and turned away rudely. But the third time she asked, she was helped.

And then at last there it was, sitting majestically amid dwellings equally impressive: the elegant four-story town house of Madame du Bois, judicial astrologer, consultant to princes and bankers and merchants and lords. And high churchmen. She should not forget the churchmen.

The town house was larger, newer, decidedly more impressive even than the house of Robert in Montigny, where she and Martin had waited for hours.

Montigny seemed, suddenly, like a very long time ago.

For quite five minutes Sylvie stood across from the house of Madame du Bois, feeling abashed. Then she forced herself to swallow her intimidation. This was, she reminded herself, Ceciline's friend. What was it Ceciline had said? "True friendship does not concern itself with the obvious."

She stepped up to the painted door and gathered her courage for an encounter with a series of indifferent servants who would doubtless stand between her and Madame du Bois.

But she did not need even to knock. As she stood, the door opened smoothly, and the tall, sturdy manservant heard her low-voiced request to see Madame du Bois with seeming tolerance. "Do you have an appointment?" he did ask. But when she shook her head—certain she would be denied, hand clutching into her pocket for the letter—he said only: "Come in." He did not ask her name or her business, did not except for one brief flicker let his eyes dwell on her clothing. Sylvie followed him inside in astonishment and sudden wariness. He walked her past two other servants, both tall and sturdy like him, and into the depths of the house.

Left alone in a perfect little antechamber, she was again conscious—for a flicker of the eyes is, after all, a flicker—of the contrast between its elegance and the scraped-threadbare poverty of her dress. She had been wearing it for weeks of travel. She brushed her skirt anxiously with her hand, and then stopped. She might dirty the exquisite carpet.

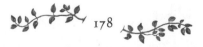 178

Too late, she thought of her shoes, and of the open sewers on the cobblestone streets through which she had walked. Had she avoided the worst? She could not sit on the intricately carved settee behind her. She must remain standing. Indeed, she scarcely dared move.

She swallowed hard against the resurgent fear, and against an abrupt consciousness of Martin's absence. She wished he were with her. Had he missed her yet? Had Robert? How long had she been gone? She felt as if she had been hours in the city streets, but of course it was not so.

Would Madame du Bois see her? Sylvie had not given the servant her letter, had not even mentioned it or given Ceciline's name as a reference.

But finally, finally, the door to the antechamber opened again. The servant bowed gracefully. "Madame du Bois," he murmured. From behind him a tall woman entered the room. Her silk skirts whispered, and her familiar beauty was more astonishing than ever, robed expensively as she was, but her eyes were as deep and gentle as before.

"You came at last, my dear," said Ceciline. "Robert is not as speedy on the road as I thought.

179

It took me only a week. But then he had so much to bring with him." She looked around the room, brows raised, laughter in her voice. "My dear, where is my little Martin? I was looking forward to seeing him once more."

At that, Sylvie did sit down upon the settee she had thought too good for her. She had to; her knees dissolved beneath her. But there was no mistake; her eyes and ears had not betrayed her. Madame du Bois, the famed caster of nativity maps in Lyon, was also Ceciline, the despised wisewoman of Montigny.

$$\backsim$$

"I don't understand," Sylvie said. Numb, she allowed herself to be swept in Ceciline's wake to a large salon. It was even more elegant than the little antechamber, its ornamentation and furnishings richly colored and delicate. The carpet was blue, thick and artfully tinted. Clouds floated across the shell-blue paint on the arched and gilded ceiling. Silverpoint etchings hung from wide blue ribbons on the silk-covered walls. Scattered chaise longues stood on tiptoe.

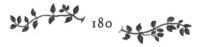

"It's not so difficult," said Ceciline. Said Madame du Bois. She had insisted that Sylvie sit. "Servants will clean," she said carelessly. She had wine served. Sylvie sipped it cautiously.

Ceciline said gaily, "In Montigny, I am Ceciline. Here in Lyon"—she gestured at the room—"I am Madame du Bois. It has been convenient, having two identities." Laughter again. Here, in this unbelievable house, she laughed and laughed, seemingly with every sentence.

"Can you guess which one of me is more respectable?" said Ceciline. "It is obvious, no? That place in Montigny! So awful." For a moment her face grew earnest. "It was becoming more and more dangerous, being Ceciline. The world has changed from your grandmother's day, my dear, and even then, it was bad enough. More than ever, women such as we—for you and I, we are alike—must use all of our wits to survive and thrive. Unless we are to live a very small life." She shrugged, smiled again. "You know to what I allude, for your grandmother was nearly executed for witchcraft and had to retreat to that tiny backwater village of yours. Not the choice

I wished to make for myself, my dear." She surveyed the beautiful room with unconcealed pleasure. One hand stroked the fabric of her gown.

Sylvie blinked at Ceciline, placed like a rare jewel in a precious setting. She had shone with warmth and kindness in her bare Montigny court-yard house; here in Lyon, she glittered. But she was still the same person, whatever she called herself. Was she not?

Why had Ceciline sent Sylvie to meet her in her second identity, as Madame du Bois? Could Ceciline not have helped her in Montigny? Could Madame du Bois help Sylvie now, here?

Did Robert know? He must, and so he had lied to Sylvie—by omission, if not in words. Her heart hardened toward him—and by this change she understood with shock that, against her will and mind both, she had allowed it to go soft.

And Martin. Had he, too, concealed things from Sylvie? It seemed possible. Martin had talked long with Ceciline in Montigny; she had told him about her friendship with Grand-mère Sylvie. Grand-mère Sylvie herself had told Martin more than she had ever told Sylvie. What did Martin know?

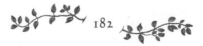

The questions formed circles and chased one another; they seeded themselves like weeds and grew again, differently. But Sylvie had to begin somewhere.

Sylvie said. "Ceciline, please do explain to me—"

"Not Ceciline, my dear," said Ceciline, smiling. "Not in Lyon. Here, I am Madame du Bois. Call me Madame."

"Madame," echoed Sylvie. With the word, she felt the Ceciline of Montigny retreat like the sky above Lyon. She cleared her throat. "Why—"

Ceciline—*Madame*—placed her hand momentarily on Sylvie's arm. "I know," she said. "You have many questions. And I promise, I shall answer. But the answers may be less important than you think.

"My dear, there is only one important question. Do you trust me?" The laughter faded completely from Madame's eyes; they were grave now, and too deep to be read. "I *do* know what's best for you, and that there is danger that you must carefully avoid. Believe me."

Sylvie took but a moment to think.

"Yes," she said steadily. "Yes, I think I must say that I trust you."

"Good," said Madame. "Your grand-mère would wish you to. You have a wondrous gift, and I can help you. I promise. But do not question my methods." Her voice was entirely sincere, and her eyes grave. "You do not have enough knowledge to question me."

The tangle of questions in Sylvie's head had only thickened.

She had trusted Ceciline of Montigny. She wished she could trust Madame du Bois.

But of course she did not. There had been too many lies, and too much concealed, and—and also she hated this elegant, elegant house.

So.

So she would withhold her trust from Madame du Bois of Lyon. But she would school her emotions and husband her questions and, for now, behave as if she did trust her.

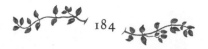

Eighteen

You came to me without even telling Robert and Martin? You left them on the quay? Oh, you have been a naughty child."

Madame du Bois seemed amused. She would, she said, immediately send a message to Robert, to tell him and Martin that all was well.

"Does Robert know?" Sylvie asked bluntly. "That you are Ceciline?"

Madame du Bois tilted her head to the side. "No," she said. "It has never seemed necessary to tell him. It was not difficult to avoid meeting him in person here in Lyon."

Sylvie was not sure whether to believe her. But she nodded. Perhaps he did not know—and so had not lied to Sylvie—but perhaps Madame du Bois simply *thought* Robert did not know. She said: "There's no need for your message. I will now return to the quay myself—"

Madame du Bois straightened. "My dear! No, you must stay here. You will be my guest. I have already picked out a room for you. What did you think? That you would sleep on the quay, as you slept on the road while traveling?" A slight frown. "Surely you are not so naive as to think that a good idea?"

"Well, but I must get back to Martin—"

"My dear, Martin is a boy. For him it is a great adventure to be here in the city, to be among men, to be doing things. Yes?"

"Yes . . ."

"Indeed." After a slight pause, Madame du Bois added gently: "As I understand it—and you will remember that Martin shared his heart with me in Montigny—Martin wished to accompany you on your journey. But perhaps it is time now for Martin to begin a journey of his own, without you. For he

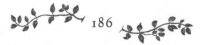

has dreams, does he not? Which are not the same as yours?"

Sylvie compressed her lips, remembering Martin's words: "I just want to see the world."

"My dear," pursued Madame du Bois, "is it right for you to ask for more from him? It is not as if he were really your brother. You cannot mean to have him stay with you forever."

That, too, was true. Sylvie fixed her eyes upon her rough hands as they clutched each other in the lap of her old gown.

Madame du Bois said gently: "You have *me* now. Let Martin go."

Sylvie reminded herself to be careful what she said. But Sylvie could not help herself. She blurted: "I don't understand who you are. I don't know what to believe. I don't even understand—what do you want from me? What do you expect? Do you—are you offering to be my teacher?"

"Yes, of course," said Madame du Bois, raising a surprised brow. "Was it not clear? I'm sorry. You will live here in Lyon with me, under my protection, and I will teach you how to manage and use your . . . gifts. *Safely.*" She looked straight at Sylvie.

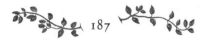 187

"I will help you," she said. "And in return, you will help me."

A bargain. Commerce.

Everything in the world: commerce.

"How long," said Sylvie, "will this take?"

Madame du Bois sighed. "From your face, one would never know that you were searching for this very situation. Desperate to find a teacher. Are you not still?"

After a moment, Sylvie nodded. "Yes."

"Of course! Because there is much for you to learn; you know this yourself. Five years, perhaps. Or seven."

Seven years: a standard period of apprenticeship. It made sense. It had been foolish of her to think otherwise.

Sylvie said slowly, "But my mother—how can I be gone so long from my mother? I thought—I had planned . . ." She stopped.

Madame du Bois's face was not without sympathy. "My dear," she said gently. "You know better than anyone that your mother will not miss you. You must learn to see this as the blessing that it is."

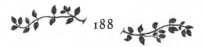

Sylvie sat very still.

"We'll talk about that again later. For now, we must discuss something far more important. Your gift." Madame du Bois turned on the settee and reached out her hand halfway to Sylvie. She held it there, saying nothing. But what she wanted was quite clear.

Sylvie's stomach roiled. For several seconds she did not move to take that hand.

Madame du Bois waited. Her eyes compelled. Those eyes scared Sylvie; she looked away nervously. She took a deep breath. But then she moved her own hand, as carefully as if it were the frailest bloom, and touched that of Madame du Bois.

Madame du Bois's two hands closed firmly over Sylvie's.

Look at me, Sylvie.

Sylvie started. She heard the words as clearly as if they had been spoken aloud. But they had not been. They pressed on her mind insistently, like fingers. She was aware of surprise. Of fear. Of the tremble of rebellion, of the impulse to snatch her hand away and run.

But she was also aware of relief. Madame du

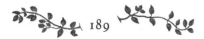

189

Bois had not lied. She, too, had mind powers. She really could help Sylvie. She could teach her!

Look at me.

Some things, if they are to be given at all, must be given blindly, Sylvie thought anxiously. Not given on faith, not given on trust, but offered in the dark, upheld on hope alone. She thought fleetingly of Robert's marriage proposal.

Then she turned her head abruptly, unaware of having even made the decision. She met Madame du Bois's gaze. She fell into it and was gripped, strongly.

She let Madame du Bois have her.

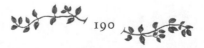

Imagine that you are a scooped handful of earth. The Hands that hold you are firm, intelligent, judicious. Perhaps a little cold. Deliberately, the Hands let a few grains of you slip between them and escape. But the rest is retained with ease, and from above, an Eye examines it and notes:

- the precise darkness of each earthen granule
- an attenuated ant that burrows industriously, oblivious of the minute flecks of glinting mica

- the rough sphere of a pebble
- the faint damp of healing water
- a seed of grass, already fated to sprout up green and strong
- other seeds, or possibilities of seeds, crammed as dense as dust

And as the Eye above sees these things, so do you. Possibly it is the first time you understand that you are not one but many, with each of the many utterly whole and individual, determined to survive. And that—as each element inside you pulses with ruthless life—the possibilities for your survival are myriad, perhaps infinite. The exhilaration of it is unspeakable.

But you are not free. There are the Hands around you, and the Eye above.

And despite your new understanding, you feel—you *are*—trapped. Helpless.

⁓

Sylvie pulled her hand away from Madame du Bois and jumped to her feet, gasping.

"My dear," said Madame du Bois mildly. "I wasn't done looking at you."

 191

"I'm sorry." Though Sylvie was not. After a moment, she managed: "Why . . . how . . . what were you *doing*?"

"Merely looking. Did it frighten you?"

There was no sense denying it. "Yes." Sylvie began to walk about the room, heedless now of its alien elegance and of the state of her shoes and her skirt's hem. She circled the settee, turned precipitately, retraced her steps. "Yes," she said again, almost as if she spoke to herself. "I could feel you . . . looking. Thinking—searching." She shuddered, unable to suppress the shivers. She whirled on Madame du Bois. "What were you looking for? What?" Even as the words left her lips she felt shamed. For she, too, had been looking for something, when she probed her mother. And Yves.

If you did not look, you would not find.

She had not known then how it felt to be probed. And even in her distress, she recognized that this was a valuable lesson.

"What were you looking for?" she said again to Madame du Bois, more calmly.

An indecipherable expression passed briefly

over Madame du Bois's face. She said: "For you, of course. Your essence. I want to know you."

"I did not like it," said Sylvie.

"I know." Madame du Bois stood up smoothly. "That is immaterial," she said. "Which is your first lesson."

Sylvie blinked.

"The first lesson," said Madame du Bois, "is about the nature of your gift. It is not likeable. With it, you will not do things that are . . . likeable." Her tone invested the word with scorn. "That is not what your gift is *for*."

Sylvie stared at Madame du Bois. She could not have understood. Madame du Bois could not have meant what Sylvie had thought, for an instant, she did mean. Hesitant, she said: "I knew . . . It has felt bad, felt like a wrong thing, when I . . . used my gift. But there must be some way to make it feel right. To—to do right with it. To use it properly—use it to do good—use it to help, to heal." She stumbled and, despite Madame du Bois's patiently raised eyebrow, tried to continue. "That is what I want to learn."

Her feet moved; she paced the room again. "I need—I want—I know—there must be some way

to use this for healing. Then it would feel right. I know it would then feel right." She spread her hands. "When you looked at me—you saw who I am. Who I want to be. Yes?"

She felt as if her soul were utterly naked. Wordless now, she looked pleadingly at Madame du Bois.

As Sylvie looked at Madame du Bois's face, she saw faintly superimposed there, in her mind's eye, for a flickering moment, the sickly tomato plant at Ceciline's house in Montigny.

"In some ways, you are very like your grand-mother," said Madame du Bois quietly.

Sylvie hunched a shoulder, obscurely angered.

"I am a healer like my grandmother, yes."

"But what if I told you," said Madame du Bois, "that yours is not a healing gift? That it never can be that?"

There was no air in the room. There was no air, and Sylvie was a fistful of earth again, and the Hands that grasped her had clenched, viciously.

"I am sorry," said Madame du Bois. Her voice came from very far away, and it did not sound sorry. "But it is so."

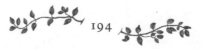

"No," said Sylvie. She said it again, more strongly. "No. I am a healer, like my mother, like my grandmother, and like her mother, too."

"Lesson two," said Madame du Bois. Was there compassion, now, in her tone? Perhaps, but mingled faintly with something else. "You are not meant to be a healer," said Madame du Bois. "That you have this gift makes it quite clear.

"You are a witch, my dear," said Madame du Bois. "Like me. And it is quite a different thing, and I am sorry, you do not have a choice."

She rose smoothly, without waiting for a response, and pulled the bell for the servant. "I see that I have shocked you, and for this I am sorry. It was necessary, however. Now you shall go to your room. Rest. I'll have a meal sent to you. And you must have a bath. Meanwhile, I shall write a note to Robert and arrange for you to say goodbye to your Martin.

"After that, your new life and your apprenticeship with me will begin."

CHAPTER
Nineteen

Sylvie panicked. She took three hasty steps forward and ran to the entry hall—only to hear Madame du Bois say from behind her in a calm, carrying voice, "Do stop her." She found herself in the firm grasp of first one and then two of the male servants.

"Your room is upstairs, my dear," said Madame du Bois with her brightest smile. "Which is in quite the other direction." She turned to the servants. "Remember my orders. You will attend her only in pairs, so that none of you are ever alone with her. And do not ever allow her to touch you for very long. That will guard against her witch-girl tricks that I have warned you of."

Witch-girl tricks. Sylvie looked at the avoidant eyes of the servants around her.

They had all been expecting her, in this house.

She was marched up three flights of stairs to a small bedchamber under the eaves. She was thrust inside, with the lock turned in the door. Her prison was luxurious in its way. Yet on sight she loathed its peach-tinted silk walls and bedcoverings and the draperies that, when pulled back, proved deceptive, covering a single tiny window set high. For light, an abundance of sweet beeswax candles stood ready. In Bresnois, the use of so many candles would have been considered wasteful, Sylvie thought. Even sinful.

Suddenly, her whole body shook. Sylvie did not think she could, unaided, have walked anywhere. Not able even to cross the small room to a chair, she leaned against the wall until the moment passed and her legs had strength again.

Then she sat, her hands in her lap, trying to think. Martin would miss her, would try to help her, but what could a child do? There was Robert,

but was he not the creature of Madame du Bois, or rather, of Ceciline?

Now she saw that Robert had warned her, if obliquely. What had he been thinking when he did so? What did he know?

After a time, servants returned. A maid brought a tray with food. Others filled a hip tub with hot water. Two maids forced Sylvie out of her clothes and took them away, leaving her only a robe. The door was locked again.

There was no reason not to bathe, Sylvie thought pragmatically, and she climbed carefully into the bath. The warm water settled around her. In other circumstances she might have liked it. Cautiously, she put her head back against the edge of the tub and stared at the ceiling. As in the salon downstairs, it was painted with a perfect oval facsimile of the sky.

The painting was framed by ornate gold trim. Sylvie closed her eyes so that she would not have to see it. Then she could stop her mind no longer.

Who was Madame du Bois to say that she understood Sylvie's nature? Sylvie was a healer! She *could* help people; she *had* helped people. She

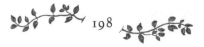

had Grand-mere Sylvie's gifts; she had Jeanne's teachings. She had healed Martin's hand. Madame du Bois knew nothing of that!

This other part of her—it could *not* be at war with being a healer. It *had* to fit. The parts of her must come together into something wholesome, though Sylvie did not herself yet understand how. But her grandmother had promised her. "Your gift is from God. You will use it in holiness, to heal, as the women of our family do."

Yet, what if Madame du Bois was right, and Grand-mère Sylvie wrong, about her nature? It did not bear thinking of, but it had to be thought of.

She wondered about Madame du Bois's position here in Lyon. Astrology was not witchcraft or sorcery, not exactly. But surely it was a borderline activity, frowned upon by the church. What did the inquisitor think? Or was he, too, one of Madame's friends, one of the high churchmen that Robert had mentioned?

Other thoughts swirled through her mind. The innkeeper saying "That Ceciline's a tricky one." Robert's distrust of Ceciline. And questions, too, about Martin. It was all very well for Madame du

Bois to say that Martin wanted to see the world, but he had no money, no protector. He couldn't go off by himself. He had left home to be with *Sylvie*.

She would have done better by Martin and herself, perhaps, if she had listened to Robert. If she had married him? No. No, Madame du Bois would not have liked that, and might have been able to do something about it, given her position. It would not have helped anything.

It was ironic. Her gift gave her access to other people's minds, but no help at all in deciding whom to trust. Or indeed, in knowing who she, herself, was.

The water had cooled. Sylvie wrapped her arms around her bare body and sank her head for a moment beneath the surface of the water. There, it was utterly silent, temptingly quiet. But when she had to, she came up again and breathed.

Breathed.

The next morning, Madame du Bois swept gracefully into the salon and beamed a smile of great kindness upon Sylvie, who had been dressed like a doll and brought there.

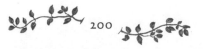

"Ah," Madame said. "I thought that dress would become you. I know, it is a bit out of style, but"—her laugh tinkled—"a huge improvement. Don't you love silk?" She stroked her own skirt with satisfaction and turned to the pair of maids. "Well done." The maids curtsied and left.

Under Madame du Bois's eye again, Sylvie managed a thin return smile. After a sleepless night, she had stood in her room for a full hour, watched surreptitiously by the maid who was making minute alterations to the fit of the silk dress while the second maid kept her eyes fixed steadily on Sylvie. Under their suspicious gazes, Sylvie had occupied herself with more mental measurement of her imprisonment. It went beyond the room, the house, the city of Lyon.

If by some miracle she could escape, what then? Would she try to continue looking for a teacher? Would not Madame du Bois chase her, with all her resources of money and connections? Would she have to run farther and farther from home, from Jeanne? Without money, protection, resources of her own? Would Martin still want to come? And what if she never found a suitable teacher?

She could not be a burden on Robert.

She wondered if she should accept the situation she was now in. She could learn *some* things from Madame du Bois. Sylvie had an almost physical memory of how it had felt to be held by the firm grip of Madame du Bois's mind. Held and searched. There *was* power there. Should not Sylvie learn about it? Learn and calmly await her chance?

She thought of this again as she brushed her hand over the borrowed silk dress and smiled falsely back at Madame du Bois. And as her mouth stretched and froze, as she looked at Madame du Bois, she knew that—even if she was giving up a chance of learning about her gift—she would leave. She would leave this house and this woman. She would leave as soon as possible and rejoin Martin. If she could. For though there was an answer here in this house, in Madame du Bois, it was not the right answer. Not for Sylvie.

Infinitesimally, she straightened her shoulders. She smiled again at Madame du Bois, and this time it was a stronger smile, and real.

She was Sylvie. She was a healer.

"You slept well?" inquired Madame du Bois.

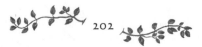

"Your room is satisfactory?" She cast a penetrating gaze over Sylvie, but it was not concerned with the questions she had just asked.

"Well enough," said Sylvie. "It is difficult in a strange place."

Madame du Bois nodded. Quick as a snake's tongue, her hands reached out as if to take Sylvie's.

Sylvie took a half step back. Before Madame du Bois could react, she said, "I've been worried about Martin. Have you received a response to the note you sent to Monsieur Chouinard?"

Madame du Bois dropped her hands. After a pause so small Sylvie might have imagined it, she said easily: "Yes. I have invited Martin here so that you may say goodbye to him. Robert will bring him."

Something in Sylvie eased a little. She said carefully, "Won't Robert—" She stumbled over the name and then switched it. "Won't Monsieur Chouinard be surprised to see you, Madame? You said he didn't know your other self." Cautiously, she stepped back again. She felt as if she were simply talking to fill the air, to keep away from those hands, that touch.

Madame du Bois laughed. She moved away a

little herself, and Sylvie breathed easier. "Robert will indeed be surprised," said Madame du Bois. This did not appear to alarm her. "But I now think it is time to tell him. I am sufficiently well established here." She moved with elegance across the room and seated herself, hands folded in her lap. She motioned for Sylvie to sit beside her. And then she waited.

Gingerly, Sylvie obeyed. She felt the tension in her shoulders and back and knew her whole body was betraying her distrust. She knew it was unwise; she knew she should pretend more ease, more acceptance. But she could not help it. She did not even want to help it. She raised her chin and said: "I don't understand how it is that Monsieur Chouinard doesn't already know. And I also still don't understand why you have two homes, two identities. Or why you sent me from Ceciline of Montigny to Madame du Bois of Lyon. It makes no sense."

In the moment she mentioned this last point of confusion, she realized: Ceciline had needed time, and the means to entrap Sylvie, if Sylvie did not

choose to stay. In Montigny, Sylvie might more easily have walked away. Her stomach clenched.

"Are you asking to understand me?" asked Madame du Bois.

"I suppose I am."

"Then I will tell you," said Madame du Bois. She held out her hands. "I will tell you in my way."

Sylvie swallowed.

"I thought you wanted to know," said Madame du Bois. When Sylvie still did not move or reply, she added softly, almost mockingly: "Lesson three. Here and now, this is your choice, Sylvie. I shall not force you. I could, and I will in future, if need be."

Sylvie thought it over. Then, deliberately, she took both her hands and clasped those of Madame du Bois.

Twenty

*O*pen your mind, said Madame du Bois without saying a word, *and I will tell you about me. And a bit about Robert, as well.*

Again, Sylvie felt the fingers on her mind. But this time they guided something to her. A river. She fell into the flow.

At first she did not recognize the boy. He was taller than Martin, but not that much older.

But when he turned, sticklike in his ragged clothes, she saw his eyes.

Robert was the best little thief in Montigny, said Madame du Bois. *And other things, too, for money. You may imagine.*

Sylvie flinched. She could not look away from the boy's eyes. She had never before seen in them this scared yet hopeful expression, but she recognized it. It lay beneath his cool, impassive, assessing adult gaze.

He was very useful to me, said Ceciline approvingly into Sylvie's mind. *I sent him on errands at first. He was very reliable. And cheap. And grateful. And, I soon realized, intelligent.*

Sylvie believed it.

Yes, Robert was smart, said Ceciline. *And it proved valuable to me in many small ways. And then . . .*

Can you understand, Sylvie, what it was to be a witch in a place like Montigny? To be alone there, after your grandmother fled, with no one to appreciate my gifts? I barely scraped a living, and in the most unpleasant ways.

Sylvie saw Ceciline's life as she remembered it.

A narrow-eyed man shuffling into her courtyard: "My cow's bewitched. Her milk's been sour for five days now. My neighbor did it! You must curse him."

A frightened, pretty young woman: "I need an amulet against the pox, for if my face is ruined, so too am I."

207

A tall, thin man who glared, put his hands on his hips, and said only: "I want to be rich."

The life of a witch, snarled Ceciline. *People coming and asking the impossible! Impossible because what they really wanted, whether they knew it or not, was an entirely different life.*

She paused, looked at Sylvie.

However, when women came on their special business, I could sometimes help. They wanted to be more beautiful. They wanted their husbands to be potent—or not. They wanted to become pregnant, or they wanted not to be pregnant.

In the parade of Ceciline's memories, Sylvie recognized with shock the landlady of the inn. She was younger, but already sure of herself. Instinctively, gently, Sylvie tried a suggestion with Ceciline—and it worked. The tiny landlady in Ceciline's memory spoke. "I can't afford children. The inn earns just enough for us to pay extra on our mortgage. We'll never be free of it with more mouths to feed." Her chin set hard. "Also, I don't want to die in childbirth."

"I can help you," said Ceciline. "It will cost you, each month."

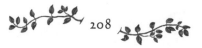

"I will pay."

"And your husband will think that you are barren."

The landlady winced, but nodded firmly. "I will do what I must do."

I worked for them all, Ceciline said. *I did my best. Even when they wanted what no one could assure, such as healthy babies or love, I tried. I boiled forty ants in daffodil juice. Do you know how hard it is to get juice from a daffodil? I soaked wool in the blood of a bat. Have you ever squeezed the blood from a bat? I cut tails off foxes. I mixed herbs with earthworms. I molded wax images. I fumigated bedchambers with the bile of fish. I prepared talismans. I muttered charms and enchantments until I was hoarse. Sometimes they seemed even to work, sometimes not. Who could tell? Meanwhile, my real gift—*your *gift—couldn't be used in this work. It was not wanted.*

Still, I did my best. I tried and tried to think like your grandmother—to think that I was helping, that I was needed. That comforting people was as important as anything else.

But it wasn't. Oh, they came and they came, and they asked and they asked. But what did they return for my labor? What did they give me? A sol or two, or a

stringy chicken! And their whispers, and their fear, and even their spit—when they thought I would not notice.

Is it any wonder I began to hate them?

Do I shock you, Sylvie? You with your saintly grandmother who never wanted anything in life but to be what she was? Who thought that being a forest woman, being a healer, was better than being what I was? I knew she thought her gifts were superior to mine. I knew she looked down on me, though she never said so. I knew. I always know what is in people's heads. And I was glad when Sylvie ran away, off to that village, away from me. I wasn't lonely, I was glad. Without Sylvie, I could finally be fully myself. I could finally think. I began to wonder if there was an easier way for me to live.

Sylvie felt the blast of emotions from Ceciline almost as if they were physical blows. She stiffened against them. Yesterday she had pulled away; she had gotten away. Today . . . Today she had already managed to manipulate Ceciline's thoughts . . .

She gathered herself cautiously. Once more, she sent a thought of her own into the flow of Ceciline's. She longed to see her grandmother, young again, in Ceciline's memories—but that was less important right now than . . .

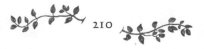

Robert, she said. *Tell me about Robert. He was useful, you said.*

Yes, said Ceciline with surprising obedience. *It was Robert who finally gave me a way out. Not that he knew what he was doing. But he showed me how I could leave Ceciline behind and become something better. Something finer. He showed me how I could become Madame du Bois.*

But—it was not so hard to guide the inner conversation after all—*but you said he does not know.*

Of course not. Ceciline's mind-tone was incredulous and faintly smug. *Why should I tell him what I truly thought, truly wanted? I told you he was smart. I've never trusted Robert, never. I used him. I did nothing that could have given him a hold over me. Don't you understand?*

Explain it to me, said Sylvie. *Robert ran errands for you?*

Any kind of errand, said Ceciline. *I was in a wonderful position, you see, knowing so much about my clients. I'd send Robert to spy out more secrets, or to collect favors for me. He'd do anything for food—for the merest scraps. And then . . .*

And then? said Sylvie, very evenly.

I had noticed he was canny. But one day it occurred to me to look in his mind. I had not bothered before. And what I saw!

Sylvie waited.

I had thought he would be thinking about food. Or nursing some grudge against one of the other boys—they used to lie in wait for him and beat him up. You know the kind of thing.

Sylvie did know. She contained herself. She waited.

But no, Ceciline continued. *Robert was thinking about peacocks! He was obsessed with peacocks—and trying to nerve himself to ask me for a favor. My dear, I was astonished.*

So was Sylvie. She asked: *Peacocks? What is that?*

She easily picked up Ceciline's mind-picture and watched several gorgeous, vain birds strut across a meticulous lawn, tail feathers stretched out spectacularly. She gasped with surprise and delight. But her bewilderment echoed the memory of Ceciline's, and she let the older woman see it.

Ceciline said: *Robert had heard—he was always hearing things—that the wife of the lord had obtained a peacock as a present from her father, who was close to*

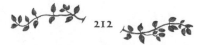

the king. Robert had gone to see it. But the lady wanted a flock—she longed for a flock; she was driving her husband crazy—and peacocks are dreadfully difficult to get, my dear. They are not native to our country.

Sylvie was lost. She felt a peculiar surge of nostalgia. Hearing this story was almost like talking with Robert himself. There was the same sensation of having taken a left when you fully meant to go right, of unexpectedly finding yourself in a place you had not known existed. It was also the way she had felt in the marketplace when the egg landed. *Go on,* she said to Ceciline, fascinated. *Why should Robert care if this lady longed for peacocks?*

He thought he knew of a peahen! said Ceciline. *And he was right, as it turned out. I never understood how he knew, for it was a straggly, leggy thing, that peahen. Really, you would not think it was of the same species as the peacock. I thought it was a deformed chicken! I was planning to wring its neck and make it into soup.*

It was yours?

Yes, said Ceciline. *Payment from a man from out of town who wanted a caul for luck. I would never have traded a real caul for what we both thought was a deformed chicken, but I had something that would pass*

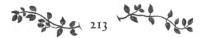

and he didn't know the difference, so I gave it to him and took the scrawny bird in exchange. Which was actually a peahen, as it turned out. I still don't know why Robert suspected. Of course he had studied the peacock carefully. He wanted to take my peahen to the lady to see if her bird would recognize a mate. He said he would do anything I wanted, if I would only give him the peahen.

You agreed?

Why not? It would be entertaining, if nothing else, and at worst Robert might get a beating, for presumption. But he was right, and the lady paid him a rich sum for the peahen. I let him keep some of it. It was our first business deal together.

I understand, said Sylvie slowly.

Do you? said Ceciline. *I think not. For after that, I read Robert's mind more carefully and found . . . all kinds of schemes. All kinds of dreams, and all to do with money and trading and so on. So I told him I would be his partner, and we would invest the profits from the peahen into another scheme of his. This one had to do with hemp. Of course I did not really think anything would come of it.*

But it did, said Sylvie. She sent the thought softly, surely.

 214

Yes, said Ceciline, the edge of remembered amazement lingering in the word. *And then he had another idea. And another. And for the first time I began to have money. Real money.*

The wonder and pleasure of that, too, was still present in Ceciline's memories.

Sylvie was by now deeply enmeshed in the story. To save her life, at that moment she would not have let go of Ceciline.

She prompted: *And then?*

Indignation. *And then I realized: What good was that money to me? What good was it to Ceciline, witch of Montigny? I could never become a rich and respected lady in that town. No one of any station would ever speak to me. Even the peasants spit on me. They would accuse me of theft, did they know of my new wealth—theft and witchcraft, and hang me or worse. No. I would need to begin again, as someone else, somewhere else. So I bided my time. I invested my ninety percent of the profits from Robert's schemes into his new business—or rather, my business, for it was my money.*

Again, Sylvie contained herself. But something of her thoughts must have escaped, for Ceciline said sharply: *Robert never complained! He was glad*

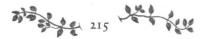

enough of my money. He'd be nothing without me, for all his sharp mind, and he knows it. I deserved that ninety percent.

Sylvie sent the same kind of soothing murmur to Ceciline that she had once used with Martin. Amazingly, it worked. *What happened next?* she asked.

Robert had started talking about Lyon and how important it was becoming. It was he who made me aware of all the people of importance who lived here. But I knew, even if I changed my name and came to live here, money would not be enough. I would need a way to make those important people want to know me, want to be my friends. I needed them to be my friends, you see, so that I could become one of them.

How odd, Sylvie thought, to hear the wail of the outcast from Ceciline. Or perhaps not, Sylvie realized. She had not been paying sufficient attention earlier, but it had been there.

Ceciline had already rushed on. *Then it came to me! I did not have to be a witch in Lyon. In Lyon, I would be an astrologer.*

You already knew how? asked Sylvie.

Oh no! Amusement, now. *My dear, surely you*

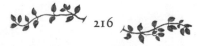

know how difficult astrology is? All those charts and maps and arithmetic calculations. I never studied it.* A tinge of bitterness now. *It's an upper-class art.*

I merely said I was a specialist in giving business advice. I took birthdays and birth times and told my clients that I would cast their nativity charts. And when they came back, I would not give them the chart itself, but instead give them advice based, so I said, on their charts, about the business decisions they should make. They did not complain. To the contrary.

This time Sylvie did not need to ask. She knew. *Robert. You got the business information from Robert, somehow. From his mind.* Before proposing to Sylvie, Robert had spoken of Madame du Bois's nativity charts. But he had not mentioned her giving business advice.

Of course Robert, said Ceciline. *He would come to me in Montigny, to report to his business partner, Ceciline, as he ought. And then Madame du Bois would give information to her own clients in Lyon. For a price, of course. But a surprisingly reasonable price, for the right people.*

The price of their friendship, and their good opinion. Sylvie understood. She thought she understood nearly everything now. She realized suddenly

that she could not risk Madame du Bois seeing how angry she was on Robert's behalf. Gently she disengaged her mind, and her hands.

She spared a momentary thought for the fact that she had to some extent at least controlled the internal conversation with Ceciline. She was not completely helpless, after all. But her thoughts were still on Robert. Did he understand the extent to which he had been used? Surely not, if he did not know that Madame du Bois and Ceciline were one and the same.

She stood up. "I am surprised at your frankness in telling me all this."

Madame du Bois frowned. She seemed ever so slightly confused by Sylvie's abrupt withdrawal. Or perhaps by the release of Sylvie's gentle hold on her mind? Sylvie wondered if Madame du Bois had meant to tell her so much. Had Sylvie made her do so?

Perhaps.

But Madame du Bois's brow smoothed rapidly. She said: "What harm can it do? You are my apprentice. Like Robert, you belong to me now. You need me, if you are to learn to manage your own mind

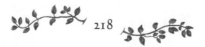

gifts, so you will do as I say. Besides, this is Lyon, not Montigny or your little village. I am powerful here. I have important friends. You could not survive here without me.

"That is lesson four," finished Madame du Bois complacently. "That you must do as I say. Just like Robert. And your little Martin, too, if I choose."

Sylvie looked back at Madame du Bois and said nothing.

She thought that Madame du Bois had already taught her quite enough.

But mixed up with her horror and anger and almost shocking determination, Sylvie felt a twinge of another emotion. This woman had had no one like Jeanne for a mother and teacher, and she had not wanted to learn from her friend Grand-mère Sylvie. It was now abundantly clear: Madame du Bois had no calling. No calling to healing, of course. But also no calling to witchcraft, no calling to astrology. No calling even to motherhood, or her relationship to Robert would have been quite different.

No calling to anything, so far as Sylvie could see.

Without a calling, you could never become. The best you could hope for was to survive.

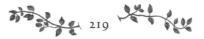

Robert had a calling of his own. It had first come to him, apparently, in the shrill of a lonely peacock, and he had been following it ever since.

Sylvie felt pity for Madame du Bois. She did not think even the best of healers—the healer she herself hoped to become—could give someone else a calling.

Not if that person did not desire to find the way to it herself.

CHAPTER

Twenty-One

"Visitors, Madame," said the maid. Sylvie looked up; could it be Martin and Robert? But they were expected only late this afternoon, and Sylvie and Madame du Bois had just finished a silent noontime meal.

Madame du Bois raised her eyebrows inquiringly.

"The archbishop," said the maid impressively. "And another gentleman from the church. I've shown them to the main salon."

"Ah," said Madame du Bois calmly. "Of course." A small, pleased smile was just perceptible on her mouth. She turned to Sylvie and, plain as day, her face said: *See what an important person I am here in Lyon? See who comes to call?*

Sylvie was reminded of Martin's expression when he caught a live fish in his hands. She felt again that stab of pity for Madame du Bois and wondered what Grand-mère Sylvie had truly thought about Ceciline. "You cannot heal everybody," Grand-mère Sylvie had said to Jeanne, and to Sylvie, often. Had Ceciline been among those in her mind?

Madame du Bois rose. "Come, Sylvie. I'll introduce you to my visitors."

Despite the new strength that she felt in herself, as she trailed Madame du Bois to the salon, Sylvie felt herself tensing. Her pity and understanding for Madame du Bois had not materially changed her situation. She was still a virtual prisoner. And meeting an archbishop . . . Sylvie did not think it was a good idea. She had never before met a churchman higher than Father Guillaume. And now she knew to take Grand-mère Sylvie's warnings to heart.

And she could not help thinking of the men from the caravan. Were they spreading rumors about her?

Nonetheless, as Sylvie hung back and watched

Madame du Bois, face wreathed in smiles, kneel and kiss the archbishop's hand, Sylvie at last felt the full force of what Madame du Bois had achieved. What a coup it was indeed for Ceciline, witch of Montigny, to greet an archbishop, clad in full impressive robes, in her home, as her friend. Sylvie's soul contracted with a mix of feelings so complex she had to stop for a moment right in the middle of the room. Across the morass of emotion floated a single sentence, one of Ceciline's: "True friendship is not about the obvious."

But she had no time to consider what to make of it.

"Madame," said the archbishop, who seemed fully as pleased to see Madame du Bois as she was to see him. "I am so glad to find you at home. I have brought a new colleague of mine to meet you." He gestured to his companion, who, in contrast with the archbishop's richly colored garments, was clad entirely in black. "Madame du Bois, this is Monsieur Lehmann, the new inquisitor, who comes to us most recently from Geneva. Monsieur Lehmann, the famous Madame du Bois, who is, I am happy to say, an excellent friend of mine and of the church."

The inquisitor.

For several seconds, Sylvie did not breathe. There was no air in the room to allow for breathing. Then she was able to hear again, the end of something from Madame du Bois.

"—my young friend, Sylvie."

Somehow Sylvie managed to curtsy. To express a greeting in tones that sounded almost normal. When the archbishop extended his hand, palm downward, expectant, she kissed it. She was aware of Madame du Bois watching her. She did not look back at her. She did, however, glance quickly at Monsieur Lehmann, the inquisitor, but could not bring herself to examine his face. She wondered if they could all see her fear.

Had Madame du Bois somehow done this on purpose to scare Sylvie? Maybe she would not escape this place after all. Maybe she could not escape. Maybe Madame du Bois was smarter than Sylvie.

The others were talking. Sylvie dared look up, covertly.

The archbishop was tall, stooped, with grizzled hair and a high, smooth, untroubled brow.

The much younger Monsieur Lehmann was shorter than Sylvie. The longest, thickest lashes Sylvie had ever seen fringed his blue eyes, but nature had compensated for that abundance with pupils tiny as fleas. Unlike the archbishop, Monsieur Lehmann had risen when they entered the room; now, at a gesture from Madame du Bois, he reseated himself, his odd gaze fully on Madame du Bois but skipping occasionally, and without discernible connection to the conversation, to the archbishop or to Sylvie. He pulled a small stone ornament from his pocket and rubbed it absently with his thumb. But he never looked down at it, seemed scarcely aware that he held it.

Sylvie sat where Madame du Bois indicated. She listened as the others talked, and gradually she relaxed a little. This appeared to be a social, or even perhaps a business, call. Madame du Bois and the archbishop—though not the inquisitor—spoke in some detail of Lyon city politics, of the city's hopes for the future of the new silk trade. "Oh, I think it will be fabulously successful," said Madame du Bois, laughing gently. "I have cast its horoscope. Invest at once!"

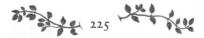

Monsieur Lehmann's hands paused briefly. The archbishop leaned forward. "Church funds, yes, of course, but do you mean—should I invest my own family money?"

"Yes," said Madame du Bois decidedly.

The archbishop frowned. "But the risk . . . you really think . . . ?"

"Invest as much as you can. In fact, borrow and invest even more."

Monsieur Lehmann spoke suddenly. "Are you borrowing money to invest, Madame?"

"I plan to do so, yes," said Madame du Bois composedly. "My Venetian bank is making arrangements."

Or Robert's, Sylvie thought sourly. She wondered if Madame du Bois's leaking of Robert's thoughts all over the city would have a bad effect on his plans. It seemed likely, for Sylvie had overheard him talking to Arnaud about the importance of an early investment, before many people understood how profitable the silk trade was likely to be.

"Ah." The inquisitor nodded. He shifted the ornament absently from one hand to the other and then back again. His gaze buzzed around the room

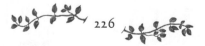

like a dayfly. His mind and his hands and his eyes all appeared to be engaged on separate business. "Rather a strange man," Robert had said. She found she trusted his opinion. It would take one strange man to know another, after all—and despite the tension of her situation, the thought almost made her smile.

"I'll do it," said the archbishop at length. He smiled warmly. "What would I do without you, Madame?"

"You would be less wealthy," said Madame du Bois genially, and the archbishop laughed aloud. Sylvie read the satisfaction in Madame du Bois, whose gaze was now turned directly on her, as if to say, *See how highly I am valued?*

The archbishop had turned to the inquisitor. "This is a marvelous opportunity for you, too, Michel. You're too new to Lyon, perhaps, to know how honored you are, to receive Madame's advice like this. You'll take it, of course. If you like, I can find you a banker."

"I have no head for business," said Monsieur Lehmann dismissively.

"But—"

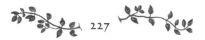

"I am a poor man, and content to be so. I have refused my family's money. My attention is not on these worldly matters." His voice was unemphatic, informational, but nonetheless there was a short, appalled silence. Apparently not content with it, Monsieur Lehmann added, just as calmly: "James 1:11."

Sylvie swallowed. The archbishop would of course understand this reference, but would Madame du Bois? Not many knew their Bible well; you needed Latin for that. And indeed, Madame du Bois was frowning, seeming uncertain.

On pure impulse, Sylvie spoke softly into the air, translating the verse into French: "For the sun is no sooner risen with a burning heat, but it withereth the grass, and the flower thereof falleth, and the grace of the fashion of it perisheth: so also shall the rich man fade away in his ways." For a moment, she could not help thinking of Robert. Monsieur Lehmann would disapprove of him too, for he was the very definition of worldly. Why didn't Sylvie disapprove any longer?

Her translation earned her a piercing glare from the red-faced archbishop. But Monsieur Lehmann

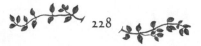

nodded at her with approval. "Yes, indeed," he said simply. "Time is short. Even a woman may know this." He lapsed into silence, fingering his stone ornament. He appeared entirely unaware of the newly cold atmosphere in the room.

Finally the archbishop broke it. "I was not aware, Michel," he said icily, "that you were a Reformer."

"Eh?" The inquisitor roused himself. "Monseigneur? A Reform—no. Why would you think that?" He frowned.

"Well," said the archbishop between his teeth, "if you find wealth ungodly, you must object to that of the church? Maybe you—"

Monsieur Lehmann waved his hand dismissively. "Don't be so illogical," he said. He leaned forward, intent yet unobservant, lashes sweeping wide but his gaze faraway. "Historically, the church has always valued poverty. The Reformers ask, has that value been reduced to lip service? Have we wandered from God? I am no Reformer, but I say, why not debate it? Why not allow the questions to be asked? What are we afraid of?" His voice rose with enthusiasm. "Perhaps we have made mistakes; we're only men, after all, and fallible."

The archbishop jumped to his feet. Knuckles white, he towered over Monsieur Lehmann. "Who sent *you* to search out heresy?" thundered the archbishop. "The pope is not fallible! I'll report you! I'll have you recalled! You're on the very brink of heresy yourself!" He stopped, breathing hard.

Madame du Bois was smiling again.

Sylvie waited, interested. She did not think that the strange Monsieur Lehmann was the kind to back down.

She was correct. Monsieur Lehmann stared back at the archbishop, his tiny pupils fully expanded. He stood up. "Oh no," he said, and for all its quiet, his voice filled the room even more fully than the archbishop's. "I understand heresy. Believe me, Monseigneur, I know it when I see it." He paused and then struck. "Heresy is not to be found in my quotations from the Bible. But, indeed, it is here in this room. Right now."

Beside her, Sylvie heard Madame du Bois draw in a sharp breath.

"This house stinks of it," went on Monsieur Lehmann to the archbishop, without glancing at Madame du Bois or at Sylvie. "Prognostications,

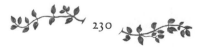

soothsaying, astrology. Micah 5:12," said the young inquisitor relentlessly. "Galatians 5:19 to 21. Consult your Bible, Archbishop, for I fear you have not done so for some time." And now he did look, with his strange eyes, straight at Madame du Bois. "Or you would not have taken me here, to meet your so-called friend. And you would not take heed of her devilish advice."

Sylvie could feel Madame du Bois trembling. But then, she was trembling herself.

Then the inquisitor's eye was directly on Sylvie. "You, girl. You with your knowledge of the Bible. Your soul is in mortal danger in this house. I warn you."

Sylvie met those strange eyes. Sudden, wild inspiration possessed her. She did not need gifts for this, only her wits. She said quietly: "Yes. I know my danger."

It surprised him. He blinked. "Beware pride," he said. "Beware vanity."

"I shall try," said Sylvie. She kept her gaze firmly on his. Her heart beat heavily in her throat. "Will you help me save my soul?" she asked.

Monsieur Lehmann was clearly taken aback.

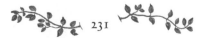

But he said directly: "Yes, of course. How may I assist?"

Sylvie said: "I should like to leave this house, as you recommend. Would you escort me now? For I fear I will not be allowed to leave otherwise."

Absolute quiet. Then Monsieur Lehmann bowed and held out his arm. Sylvie rose and took it. She did not look at Madame du Bois, or at the archbishop. Smoothly, on the arm of the inquisitor of Lyon, she walked out of the salon, and down the corridor past the servants, and out of the house of the astrologer Madame du Bois, friend of archbishops . . . but not, it seemed, of inquisitors.

Twenty-Two

Of course, Sylvie reflected as they walked back through the Croix-Rousse toward the quays, if he knew her better, the inquisitor would be her enemy too. The witchcraft warnings in Micah and Galatians applied every bit as much to Sylvie as to Madame du Bois.

But, Sylvie thought, I am a healer, not a witch. And I shall, in the future, be careful about how I help. I did not ask for my gifts, which Grand-mère Sylvie assured me come from God, and I do not put myself above God.

But such subtleties might not matter to this strange, fearless, fanatical man. He might be sorry when he signed her execution orders—possibly—but he would sign them nonetheless, and with a steady hand and a clear conscience. She sighed and, noticing, Monsieur Lehmann smiled at her encouragingly. "I will have you back with your brother soon," he said.

She had told him about Martin, and he had asked no more; he seemed to have no personal interest, no curiosity whatsover, about her. He had not even questioned her about Madame du Bois or about her presence in Madame du Bois's house, though he had inquired into her religious training and listened intently as she described her lessons with Father Guillaume. "Your priest refers to the Gospel of Luke," he said pedantically. "It is understood that Mary chose well when she had the chance to learn from our Lord rather than perform household chores with her sister Martha."

"I have been privileged to learn from Father Guillaume," said Sylvie.

The inquisitor smiled at her vaguely, chasing his own thoughts now, and said: "We have merely a few more streets."

Her hand was on his arm. She had learned

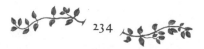

something of delicacy from Madame du Bois. She could . . . On impulse, Sylvie peeked, quickly, gently, at Monsieur Lehmann's mind.

It was a place of order, ruthlessly arranged into neat packets. The known and unknown. Good and evil. A rare mind: sure of itself. And, she thought, because of its order, it was a mind both dangerous and achingly vulnerable. Life was not generally orderly, or kind to those who expected order from it. But perhaps life would be kind to this man. She did not know whether to hope so, or not.

At least she knew better, now, than to interfere with his mind. That way lay Madame du Bois.

It was odd. She could see how dangerous this man could be to anyone who could not or would not meet his personal—though he would deny that they were personal—moral standards. But she could not help admiring him somewhat anyway. He was intelligent, passionate. And she doubted that he had ever made a pretense in his adult life. Politics, diplomacy, caution: he would have no use for these.

She hoped she would never, ever meet him again in her life. But she would be surprised—quite surprised—if she did not hear tell of his doings.

There, just ahead, was the Quai Saint-Antoine. She recognized the barges that belonged to Robert. Soon she would see him, and Martin. Her heart lifted. She turned to the inquisitor.

"Monsieur Lehmann, I thank you for your help," she said formally. "You are a brave man. I fear that the archbishop will not forgive you for your bluntness. And Madame du Bois will be quite angry as well, and I understand that she is very powerful in Lyon."

"I spoke the truth," said Monsieur Lehmann. "Truth is greater than the archbishop. As to this Madame du Bois, if she has power, it is the power of Satan, and Satan shall be defeated." He smiled at Sylvie gently and with utter sincerity. "Do not fear," he said. "Put your faith in God and our Lord, do always what you know is right, and banish fear."

Sylvie looked into the inquisitor's strange, strange eyes. It was good advice. She said, "Monsieur, I promise."

⁓

Robert's men were loading goods steadily onto barges; though the pile yet to be packed in and tied on was somewhat diminished, even Sylvie could

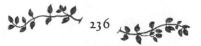

see that they had not made nearly enough progress to meet the schedule Robert had been so intent on. Anxious, she scanned the quay. She wasn't looking forward to telling Martin about Ceciline. He would mind. He would mind terribly.

As to Robert . . .

She spotted Arnaud and waved. Seeing her, his face lit up, and then he scowled. She smiled, picked up her skirts, and ran toward him. "Hello!"

He reached out as if to hug her, and then his arms dropped. "I'm mad at you," said Arnaud truculently. "We all are. Going off like that. Not a word. We searched all the streets, over and over. We were all so worried . . . Stuff can happen here to girls, it's dangerous." He rubbed his face. "You should've known, Sylvie. It wasn't only stupid. It was mean. Mean to Martin; he was so worried. And the rest of us, too, and to him—Monsieur Chouinard."

"Arnaud's right," said a voice, almost shrilly. Sylvie looked up. Yves. Yves, and the rest of Robert's men—not only those who had been on the journey from Montigny, but also the others who had joined them here to help with packing the barges. All of them looking at her, their faces still. "We were very

worried about you," said Yves, with whose mind Sylvie had interfered. "Some of us searched all night."

"I—I . . ." Sylvie stuttered. She scanned all their faces. She could barely take it in, barely understand. She had never thought . . . never dreamed . . .

"I'm sorry! I thought there was a note sent, about where I was?"

Arnaud said, "Not until—"

Bristling, Yves cut in. "Not until this morning. There was a note from that woman, that du Bois." He spat; Sylvie thought briefly that Ceciline would be distressed to know that people spat at her new identity, as at the old. "Nothing from you. If you were *my* sister, I'd beat you till you couldn't stand up. I'd have done it long since."

"I—I am sorry. Thank you," she said to Yves.

Incredibly, he flushed. "Imbecile," he muttered.

"Thank you," she said clearly to Arnaud, to all of them. "I'm so sorry. I was very wrong. Very stupid and inconsiderate." She glanced sidelong at Yves. "An imbecile, in fact. Thank you for looking for me. I don't know how to thank you . . ." Seeing their

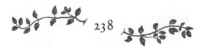

faces now, she wanted to cry. They had worried. They had looked. They had cared.

Perhaps they did not hate and fear her.

"Well," said Arnaud awkwardly, seeing her emotion. "Really, it's him you should thank. Yesterday, as soon as he realized you were gone, he ordered everyone to stop packing and look for you instead. Even though it means we'll be late to Marseille." His smile was lopsided. "Though a few of us would have looked for you anyway, orders or no."

Late to Marseille. It was an odd way to measure caring, perhaps, but no less real for that.

Sylvie drew in a breath.

"Well. We have to get back to work," said Arnaud. "So we're not even more late." The men started to disperse.

"Wait," said Sylvie. "Tell me—where is Rob— Monsieur Chouinard? And Martin?"

"They'll be back soon," said Arnaud. "Since you're here and not there. In fact, you just missed them; they set off half an hour ago to fetch you."

Here and not there. She was not fully herself; it took a moment. Arnaud had already turned to

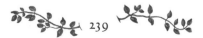

go. She called after him anxiously. "Arnaud, where exactly did Monsieur Chouinard and Martin go?"

He turned back. "Why, to her house," he said. "The house of that woman who sent the note. The astrologer, what's her name. Du Bois."

Twenty-Three

Sylvie caught her breath. "Oh no."

Arnaud saw her face and sighed. He glanced back toward the wharf, clearly impatient to get back to work. With Robert away, he was in charge of the loading process. "Don't worry about it. As soon as they find you're not there, they'll turn around and come back." When Sylvie's frown did not lift he added with a tinge of exasperation: "Look, girl. Robert is a grown man—smarter than most twice his age. He'll take care of your Martin. They'll be back soon enough."

It was good sense, Sylvie knew. But the hollow feeling in the pit of her stomach was growing. "I think I should go after them," she said.

Arnaud frowned. "There's no need."

"But that woman—"

"Go racing off again by yourself? I won't let you. Robert would have my head, and he'd be right."

"You don't understand that woman," said Sylvie. "Let me explain . . ." But she had no explanation that would make sense to him. She could not talk of mind-reading powers, and she had no right to discuss Ceciline's relationship with Robert. Silenced, she clenched her hands in frustration.

Arnaud glanced again at the wharf. "You'll stay right here. Make one move away and I'll detach one of the men from loading to watch you." He added under his breath, "We're so far behind schedule anyway, it would hardly matter."

Sylvie persisted: "But what if they don't come back soon?"

"They will."

"Suppose they're not back in an hour?"

"They will be. But if not, then I'll reconsider," said Arnaud. "Will that do?"

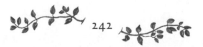

"Yes," said Sylvie reluctantly. He might be right; she hoped so. She promised to stay put, as Arnaud would not leave her until she did, and then she sat, again, by the wharf. This time she watched not the loading, but the nearest entry to the wharf area from the street. She watched and she watched as the seconds slowly accumulated into minutes and the minutes even more slowly crawled toward an hour.

Just as she was ready to jump up and tell Arnaud she must go, she spotted Robert rapidly making his way toward her, paying no heed to the throngs of people on the wharf. Not just rapidly—urgently. She rose, hand at her throat.

Martin was not with him.

Like her, Robert now wore fine city clothes, with a surcoat that featured heavy, slashed, embroidered sleeves. Deep-blue pleated silk peeked through the slashes. But mud clung to his shoes, and above the high neck of the surcoat, his face was carefully blank.

Even in the beginnings of renewed panic, she was reminded of that moment in the marketplace after Martin had thrown the egg, when Robert's cool gaze had swept comprehensively over everyone.

This time, it was Sylvie he saw amid all the other people; Sylvie upon whom he focused. And this time, she understood that there was emotion behind that impassive gaze, emotion he had learned to keep safely concealed. She thought of the child she had met in Ceciline's memories, the boy Robert who was in some ways not unlike Martin, and who should have been even more like him. However, Martin—even with his impatient father—had been more fortunate in family than Robert.

Robert had had only Ceciline.

Robert stood before Sylvie now. Sylvie looked up into his eyes. Her lips formed Martin's name, but she did not need to ask aloud.

"She wants a trade," Robert said. Though his voice was level, the word *she* sounded like an obscenity. It told Sylvie much, including that Robert now knew that Ceciline and Madame du Bois were the same person.

"You for Martin," Robert added.

Sylvie was surprised only for a moment. She nodded. Her panic ebbed a little, just knowing Martin was safe. She was able, even, to smile grimly. "Will you escort me to her house, then? I shall trade."

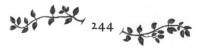

Anyone else would have asked her if she was sure. But anyone else would have used more than seven words to explain both the situation and what he thought of it. "Yes," said Robert. He had not even glanced over at the wharf or his men. He held out his arm, and Sylvie took it.

He said three more words as he efficiently steered Sylvie through the maze of city streets and the throngs of other people scurrying by on their own business. "She owns me," he said flatly, and did not look at Sylvie as he said it.

It was the one thing he had not told her in his seven words: whose side he would be on, and why. Sylvie did not look at him, either. She made her counterargument evenly: "She owned a boy called Robert. Is that boy still you?"

The warm muscles of Robert's arm, palpable beneath her hand, stiffened. For the briefest moment, his eyes met hers. Yes, there was emotion behind them—agony. *Stop*, it said.

She did not stop. He needed to know how much she knew. "What she owns is ninety percent of your business. That is different from owning *you*." She did not explain how she knew these details.

She did not say *I need your help.* She did not say *Please.*

Between Sylvie and Robert, it had come to be that very few words sufficed to say all that was needful.

Under her touch, the muscles of his guiding arm had relaxed. She had done nothing with her mind to calm him. He was controlling himself, using all the skills of his twenty-four years. A short lifetime for some, but long—she now understood—for him.

If she could have used her gift to rip Ceciline and all that she had done, and all that she was, from this man's soul, Sylvie would have. Not for her own sake, but for his. She knew better, however. It was the last lesson that Jeanne had taught her, that she could not heal by removing the thing that caused pain, not when it was connected to so many other things, things that were important.

But she wondered: Could she use her gift to change something *in* Robert? Something to help her and Martin right now? Just as—though she had known it was wrong—her tampering with Yves had helped? Yves had not gone running to the inquisitor about Martin's hand. Sylvie had stopped him.

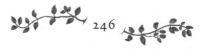

She could be more deft with her gift now. She had learned some things from her brief time with Madame du Bois, if not the things Madame du Bois had intended. Her hand was on Robert's arm. She could—so easily—reach in and attempt to influence him. Perhaps she could simply make him see that his business, all these material goods and money, was not so important.

For Robert was the key to Madame du Bois's wealth and position, to all that mattered to her. She would surely choose to keep Robert before she would choose to keep Sylvie. Choose to keep wealth and her important friends and her position in Lyon. Robert could offer Madame du Bois that choice.

If he would.

If Sylvie explained it to him, mind to mind, she could change him. She could persuade him to value position and goods and his reputation less. She could flood his chivalrous mind with her desperation. She could overpower his fear of Ceciline. She could suppress whatever made him think he was owned and helpless.

Her hand was on his arm—she would just *look* . . .

Sylvie reached out delicately and felt his mind, contorted in thought. He was thinking over what she had said about the boy Robert. There was an edge of desperation in him; he understood completely what she had omitted saying.

He had not needed to be told *You are no longer a boy.* He did not need to be told *You should choose who deserves your loyalty.* He did not need to be told *Souls are more important than money.* He already knew those things. He wanted to help Sylvie and Martin. He longed to do so. But he was afraid—afraid at a level deep and beyond even the reach of his own formidable reason.

It was simple, really. The child Robert was afraid of Ceciline. All Sylvie need do was reassure that child so that the adult Robert—competent, strong, and capable Robert—could take over. Sylvie could do that—oh, she could, so easily. And if she did, she would be doing Robert a favor. She would be freeing him, not manipulating him.

Healing him.

Yes?

"Here we are," said Robert in a voice that

sounded quite dead. He let go and crossed his arms. "Do you still want to go in?"

Sylvie felt the absence of his support as she faced the elegant four-story town house of Madame du Bois. She searched Robert's face and knew if she reached out, he would take her hand. And then she could touch him and change him.

She kept her hand to herself. She clenched it in her skirt.

He said, "I'll come in with you. Martin will need somebody. I could get him home later on, after Marseille."

"Yes," said Sylvie. "Thank you."

He hesitated. "I'll come back. I promise you I'll come back for you, later, after I have attended to my business. And I will take care of Martin meanwhile. I promise."

His repetition was a mark of how disturbed he was. She wanted to cry for him. He would hate that.

She said, "Let's go inside."

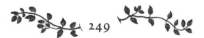

CHAPTER

Twenty-Four

Madame du Bois was seated straight-backed on one of her elegant chairs. Sylvie ignored her. "Martin!"

He stood in the very farthest corner of the salon. His face and hands were filthy, his clothes hopelessly rumpled. At his feet a vase lay smashed into several pieces. Seeing Sylvie, his face lit. Then he scowled. "You shouldn't have come. Never let anybody make you do anything."

Helplessly, Sylvie laughed. She moved from Robert's side and scooped Martin up in her arms. She hugged him as tightly as she could. She whispered to him, "I chose to come," and though she couldn't see it, she felt his relief in the way he clung to her.

He said, "Sylvie, put me down! Down!" and kicked a little. But it was just for effect. His arms around her were just as tight as her own around him.

Sylvie pretended not to know that Madame du Bois's eyes were on them. She would hold Martin just as long as she wanted to. However, after a little time, she did reset him on his feet. She knelt and looked right at him. "I've missed you so much, Martin," she said. "And I'm sorry for going off without you. Forgive me."

Martin edged a look over her shoulder.

"Ignore her," said Sylvie in a clear, calm voice. "She doesn't matter at all."

Martin's lashes fell. Then he looked right into Sylvie's eyes and whispered, "It's my fault. I liked Ceciline. I trusted her."

"So did I," said Sylvie. She refused to lower her voice for Madame du Bois's benefit. Martin, however, was still whispering. "Grand-mère Sylvie told me something . . ." He paused, mouth twisting. "Something to tell you when I thought you needed

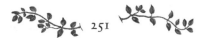

to hear it. I just didn't know when that would be. I didn't understand what she meant. So I didn't tell you in Montigny; instead I waited."

Sylvie froze. Then she clutched Martin's shoulders and dropped her voice to match his.

"What, Martin? What did Grand-mère Sylvie tell you?"

As Martin opened his mouth, Madame du Bois's hand came down on Sylvie's back. "A moving reunion scene. But overlong."

Even through the cloth of Sylvie's dress, the hand was cold. Sylvie twisted away quickly. She didn't want Madame du Bois touching her, or Martin, or Robert, who stood silent and grim near the doorway. How often had Ceciline touched Robert in the past, to rob his mind? Often and often and often.

Robert spoke decisively. "Ceciline, I won't help you with this. No more. I've decided. I'm going to take both Sylvie and Martin and leave."

Sylvie caught her breath. She stared at Robert's inscrutable face. All on his own, without any push from her, he had decided to do this.

Something in her took wing.

Madame du Bois looked surprised, but not

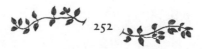

252

alarmed. One brow lifted. "Oh? Really?" she said to Robert.

Sylvie found herself silently reciting Psalm 24, which was Jeanne's favorite. *Domini est terra et plenitudo eius orbis et habitatores eius.*

Robert was focused on Madame du Bois. He said, "This is madness, Ceciline. You had me when I was a child. And now you have me still. It's enough. I will not allow you to control anyone else."

"It's not enough," said Madame du Bois, her voice entirely reasonable. "Sylvie can do things for me that you cannot. I need her. And it's for her own good." She looked momentarily at Sylvie. "It's true, my child. You know it is."

Sylvie shook her head.

The gesture seemed to infuriate Madame du Bois. "Stupid girl! Didn't you pay attention this morning? The only way to survive, with your gifts, is to do as I have done—take your power and use it. Make powerful friends. Be somebody! Do you hear me? If you go your own road, you'll end up burning! I don't need to be a seer to see that! The only reason your grandmother did not burn was because of me! For that alone, you ought to belong to me!"

"No," said Sylvie. "I belong to myself." She looked straight at Madame du Bois.

Madame du Bois's eyes narrowed. "Oh, your new friend Monsieur Lehmann will light the match himself as soon as he learns what you are. I can make sure he learns. And I will, if you don't do as I say. I shall make sure he finds out how you healed Martin's hand."

Sylvie inhaled sharply. She couldn't help it; she glanced at Martin.

"I didn't tell her," Martin said urgently. "Sylvie, she held my hands and then she looked at the right one and she just knew—"

"He'll burn with you," added Madame du Bois. There was a brief silence.

"I'm sorry," said Martin to Sylvie.

"It's not your fault," said Sylvie tiredly. Her mind had gone blank; she felt almost sick with the abrupt loss of hope.

She looked at Robert. He had tried. He really had.

But he was still entirely focused on Madame du Bois. "Don't forget me, Ceciline," he said. "I was

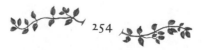

there when Sylvie healed Martin's hand. You were not. I'll deny it ever happened."

Madame du Bois's lip curled. "You're nobody," she said contemptuously. "I own your business. I am the rich one, the important one. I have merely allowed you to look as if you were. But when people know the truth, when they see the legal papers about who owns the business, what you say will not be believed."

Robert was silent.

Sylvie said to him: "No. It may be her money, but all the ideas were yours. The work was yours. It's all you; she told me so herself. She's the one who'd be nothing without you."

Robert met Sylvie's eyes. "Thank you," he said, very gently. "But you miss the point. What I, or you, see—what we know—is not important. It is what the world thinks that matters. What the lawyers say. The world will believe her."

"Who cares for the world?" The words came from the very center of Sylvie's being.

"We do." It was Madame du Bois, arrogant. "We do, Robert and I. But you are your grandmother all

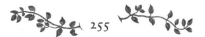

over again. Worse! She chose to escape reality in a backwater village. But you—you're going to choose death. For you and the boy." Her face changed then, softened. "I can help you, Sylvie. Let me. Choose me. For even if I do not tell Monsieur Lehmann, your way will lead to death in the end. Oh, there was a time when people respected wisewomen, to some extent at least. That day is now gone. Only women healers like your mother—those without powers—will survive in the world as it is now. And then only perhaps."

"That's true, Sylvie," said Robert gravely. He hesitated and then said: "But her way—it's not the only way to survive."

"Oh, really?" said Madame du Bois.

He ignored her. He spoke only to Sylvie. "You could marry. Behave ordinarily. Have children. Appear . . ." He paused. "Appear normal."

Sylvie met Robert's gaze. She was overpoweringly aware that of the four of them in that room, only he and she knew of his previous proposal. And that he was, obliquely, renewing it. Here. Now.

She said steadily: "And never heal? Never do what I can do?"

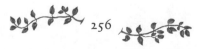

"Perhaps sometimes. In private. With family. When it's safe."

Sylvie closed her eyes. Her forehead throbbed. She heard Madame du Bois say sharply: "Nonsense! Not to use one's gifts, that's worse than death! What if I told you, Robert, that you could not be a merchant? That you couldn't scheme and trade and make money?"

It was a good point, Sylvie thought behind closed eyes. Even though she also thought that if she heard one more thing from either of them, her head would burst open like a smashed gourd.

Then Martin's high, piping voice rose above the others' and, miraculously, silenced them.

"Grand-mère Sylvie said—" Martin began.

Sylvie snapped her eyes open. Martin was beside her, licking his lips nervously. He said to Sylvie, "She said I should tell you when you were facing a big choice. I wondered if maybe I should have told you back in Montigny, when we decided to come here to Lyon. But I wasn't sure what it meant, so I didn't say anything then . . ."

Sylvie managed to say, "Tell me. If there was ever a time I would want her advice, this is it."

Martin nodded. Behind him, she could see Madame du Bois and Robert, as riveted on Martin as she was. But Martin looked only at Sylvie. "It was when she told me that I could choose to come with you. She said that I was someone special. She said—" He closed his eyes and recited the rest sing-song, as if he had memorized it word for word.

"She said, 'Martin, every person on this earth is unique, with special God-given gifts that are meant to be used. But even after you discover who it is God means you to be, you must work hard every day to become that person. You must choose and re-choose every day, because the easier road is to let the world choose who you are, and the world knows nothing of your gifts.'" Martin raised his chin and, for all his grubbiness, looked for a moment astonishingly self-possessed. He finished: "'You must never choose to be other than who you are.'"

The words fell into a little pool of silence in the room. And although it was Martin's voice that said them, Sylvie imagined she could hear her grand-mother echoing the words: *You must never choose to be other than who you are.*

Madame du Bois broke the silence. "Well, isn't

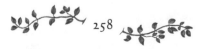

that just like Sylvie! Mystical nonsense! You can be whoever you choose to be!" Her voice was indignant, as if Grand-mère Sylvie's words were a personal attack.

Perhaps they were. Sylvie remembered what she had thought earlier: that Ceciline had no calling, no understanding of what she should do with her gift.

But perhaps Ceciline had had a calling and decided to ignore it.

She said aloud what she had always known: "I am a healer." She looked at Madame du Bois. "Not a witch." And she looked at Robert. She did not say *Nor a normal wife,* but she knew he understood.

"Then you can't be anything else," said Martin reasonably. "You have to be a healer."

Robert's face was tight. He said to Martin: "No matter the cost?"

"What?" said Martin.

"Did this Grand-mère Sylvie say that the choice must be made regardless of the cost?"

"She didn't say anything about cost," said Martin.

Robert Chouinard, the merchant, who was

259

also the boy who had noticed a yearning peacock, turned to Sylvie. "There is always a cost," he said evenly. He did not say *It might be your life.* But Sylvie understood what he meant.

"Yes," said Sylvie. She stood. She could almost feel Grand-mère Sylvie's presence, hovering, comforting. Maybe it was simply that she felt at peace. Strong. "There will be a cost. But I don't know what it will be. Nor do you."

"There are costs in life that are too high. I know what I am speaking of."

Sylvie looked at him and saw the boy Robert. She heard Ceciline telling her, "Robert was the best little thief in Montigny. And other things, too, for money." Sylvie said, not without difficulty: "The costs that were too high—were you being yourself when you paid them? Your true self?"

Why had she ever thought him inexpressive? "No," he said finally. "It took time to become myself. Time and, I will be frank, money." The silence between them was deep, and full of more questions. Sylvie lowered her eyes.

She turned to Madame du Bois, who was breathing quickly, her expression angry but oddly

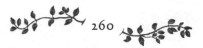

internal. Her fists were tight. Perhaps she was conducting a debate, an old debate, with herself. Or with Grand-mère Sylvie. "Madame," said Sylvie gently, respectfully.

Madame du Bois focused upon her.

"I am going to leave here," said Sylvie clearly. "With Martin, and with Robert, I am going to leave this house, and Lyon. You cannot stop me. You can call Monsieur Lehmann with your accusation of witchcraft. Perhaps you can have me killed. That will be your choice. But I will always choose to leave, as I chose earlier today. As I choose now."

After a pause, she added gently: "I cannot be what you want. You do not need me, not really. But know this also: you have helped me. Things may not be as you wanted them to be, but you have helped me nonetheless, and for this, I thank you."

Madame du Bois's lips tightened. She said: "You are just like your grandmother."

"I hope to be like her," said Sylvie quietly.

"Get out of here, then!" said Madame du Bois. "Get out!"

Sylvie would not have dared say another word. She nodded to Martin and they started toward the

door. But Robert lingered. "Ceciline," he said. "*Will* you report Sylvie to the inquisitor?"

Madame du Bois went still. A calculating light entered her eye. "I might have to, Robert," she said. "We had a very uncomfortable meeting here this afternoon, thanks to Sylvie. The inquisitor must be made to like me, to trust me. Giving him Sylvie might do the trick."

Sylvie turned back and looked carefully at Madame du Bois. Then she smiled. She felt, suddenly, almost lighthearted. She said: "No, Madame. The inquisitor will never like you. But it might not matter; your friend the archbishop might get the inquisitor transferred, for he won't want to give up your business advice." She slid her eyes to Robert and waited.

He did not disappoint her. "Business advice?" His abrupt frown interrogated Sylvie. "What business advice has she been giving the archbishop?"

"Well," said Sylvie cheerfully. "Today, she told him to invest in silk production here in Lyon. She said to sink as much money into it as possible, even to borrow if he had to."

Steam practically exploded from Robert's ears.

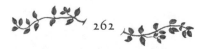

"In the name of God, Ceciline!" he yelled. "That's what I'm doing! Wait. Wait, wait, wait." He stared at her. He added slowly, "How did you even know that? I told you about the silk being transported, but not about the importance of investing as much as possible."

"She reads your mind," said Sylvie. "Then she tells others."

Robert looked like he had been stabbed. He stood still and silent for what felt like a very long time. He looked at Madame du Bois and she looked at him. Sylvie thought that Madame looked—at last—nervous.

Finally, Robert said heavily, "Nativity maps?"

"I could not learn to do them, it turned out," said Madame du Bois.

"So instead, you have been leaking my plans all over the city."

"To a select few of my trusted clients."

More silence as Robert controlled himself.

"I would have thought it obvious what a bad idea that is. Everybody will want to get in on this—it'll drive prices up—I'll be able to afford fewer shares—our business will own a smaller percentage.

 263

It might even ruin the whole venture if there are too many fingers in the broth from the start!" Only at the end did his voice rise.

Ceciline du Bois drew herself up proudly. "The archbishop expects my help," she said. "I'm happy to give it. It's an excellent business idea, too, to stay on his good side."

Robert had begun to pace the room. "Excellent business idea," he sneered. "Oh, really? Even if it ruins us? Besides, it's *my* help you're giving the archbishop—not yours!"

"It's *my* business. Ninety percent. I'll do as I please."

"The way you're going, you'll own ninety percent of nothing!"

"Don't shout in my home, Robert," Ceciline warned. "This is not the gutter."

Sylvie glanced at Martin. His eyes flew from Robert to Madame du Bois and back as they continued to argue. Robert was still pacing furiously. Madame du Bois had drawn herself up very straight and stiff. Their faces were red. They were both shouting now, about the need for trust. Trust, when neither of them had an ounce of it.

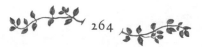

Sylvie placed a hand discreetly over her mouth so that she would not laugh openly. She knew it was not funny, or ought not to have been. And she feared that if she started to laugh, she might never stop.

It had, after all, been a very strange day.

Robert began to calm. "You have to stop it, Ceciline. You're not wrong about staying on the archbishop's good side, but you can't bankrupt us in the process. Moderation, have you ever heard of that? Let me think a minute."

"Fine," snapped Ceciline. "Figure the angles. It's all you're good for. You have no idea how much I have been helping our business all along, with my friends here in the city able to smooth our way behind the scenes. I'm glad you know at last! My position brings a lot of value! I demand credit for it!"

Robert glared one last time. Then he scrubbed at his face. Paced the room once, twice, thrice.

"Well?" said Ceciline.

"I'm thinking." Then: "Very well, Ceciline. I'll feed you information that'll be helpful to the archbishop but that won't do us much damage if made

public. Or"—his eyes narrowed, and then he suddenly grinned, like a wolf—"that will actually help us if made public. Some strategic leaks, at just the right moments. Well? What do you say, Ceciline? You have to agree not to give advice that I don't tell you to share."

"But there are other people," said Ceciline, "besides the archbishop, that I want to help."

"How many?"

"Six or so."

"That many?"

"Yes."

"Huh. It's a lot—too many, maybe." Robert paced the room again, then stopped and looked up. "We need balance. Is there anyone you want to do dirt to?"

Beside her, Sylvie felt Martin give off a little choked noise. Was he suppressing laughter now, too? She aimed a reproving glance at him and opened her mouth to raise an objection. Then she thought better of it. This was between Robert and Ceciline.

"Oh yes," said Ceciline, eyes glinting. "Oh, but yes."

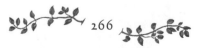

"Excellent. We can balance out the good information with bad."

Ceciline nodded. "I'll agree to that."

"And one more thing," said Robert. He had stopped pacing and now stood stock-still in the center of the room. His eyes were blank again.

"Yes?" Ceciline had relaxed.

"Fifty-fifty, from here on."

"No," said Ceciline.

"Yes." Robert was matter-of-fact. "Or I'll take my ten percent and start my own business without you. It'll take me a few years to get back to where we are now, but I can do it. Whereas without me, you'll be hard put to maintain your capital."

Robert was choosing to be fully himself now too, Sylvie thought. And that self was both canny and kind.

He was free.

There was a long, long silence. "Sixty-forty," said Ceciline.

"Fifty-fifty."

Another long silence.

"We'll discuss it," said Ceciline. "When you return from Marseille."

"No," said Robert. He smiled his wolf smile again.

There was a long pause.

"Oh, very well," said Ceciline pettishly. "Fifty-fifty."

"I will send the lawyer," said Robert.

Twenty-Five

In the dark, they walked through the city. Sylvie held Robert's arm; Martin walked independently on his other side. Robert's side, not Sylvie's. She felt a little bereft, but only a little. Martin was growing up before her eyes.

It came to Sylvie that she had come farther from home than she had ever thought to come but still had found no teacher. That she had no notion of what she would do tomorrow to begin, again, on the search. But a sliver of the moon glowed faintly far above the city, and she walked beneath it, free to choose her own future. Right now, it seemed enough. More than enough: a miracle.

Eventually Robert spoke. "It's mundane, but they'll be waiting for me—for us—at the quay. I still need to leave for Marseille early in the morning."

"Can we come?" said Martin. "Both of us?"

There was a short silence. "I think it's a good idea," said Robert. "Sylvie, you should get out of Lyon. Just in case. Come to Marseille. See the sights. You can both make—other decisions—later."

Sylvie was very tired.

"Come on, Sylvie," said Martin. "Let's go. I want to travel by river. I want to look at the sea."

His voice was eager. Robert's logic seemed faultless. Why not let someone else make this decision? Why not give herself some time, safely, to decide her immediate future?

"Yes," said Sylvie, and she was surprised at the relief that flooded through her. They were leaving Lyon.

She was with friends.

That night, Sylvie shared a room with Martin in a little inn by the quay. "I love you, Sylvie," said

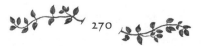

Martin sleepily. "I'm glad we're going to Marseille."

In the darkness, Sylvie smiled. "I know. But Martin . . ."

"What?"

"Don't you miss Bresnois? Don't you miss home?"

For a whole minute Martin did not reply, and Sylvie feared he had fallen asleep. But then he said quietly: "A little. I'd like to visit. But Sylvie? I don't want to live there anymore. I don't think—I don't think I would choose it."

Sylvie bit her lip. She thought of her cottage. Of Jeanne feeding wood into the hearth. Of Jeanne's eyes that last morning, smiling politely, unrecognizing, into hers. "Don't you miss your family?" said Sylvie.

"Yes," said Martin patiently. "That is why I would visit."

For a very long time Sylvie listened to him sleep. She closed her own eyes. But her mind would not let her rest.

She listened instead to Robert's and Arnaud's voices, seeping through the thin walls of the room next door. At one point they seemed to have an

argument, but she could not make out the words. She did not really try. She found herself wondering about money. She still had none. How much did Robert have? What was ten percent? What was fifty? Did she owe him money? No, she decided. She had helped him get from that ten percent to fifty, after all. Perhaps he owed her. She smiled.

Then she wondered about some other things.

When she heard Arnaud leave, she got up, dressed quietly, slipped out of her own door, and knocked at Robert's. Staring up at him, Sylvie felt exceedingly awkward, but Robert did not seem surprised to see her. He rubbed one arm across his eyes and smiled wryly.

"Couldn't you sleep?"

"No . . ." Sylvie hesitated. "Could we talk? Unless—I'm sorry. You were up last night, too. I haven't even thanked you for that. For looking for me. For your concern."

He made a motion with the flat of his palm, as if to push her words away. At length he said, "I could use a walk. Is Martin asleep?"

"Yes."

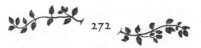

"Then let's go. You've got a shawl? Good."

Outside, Robert led her over the bridge, across the Saône, and along the river on that side, toward the cathedral. He did not, this time, offer Sylvie his arm; she walked silently beside him, wanting to speak but not sure how to begin. She was glad of Grand-mère Sylvie's shawl; in the cool night air, she pulled it closer about her shoulders. She thought again of her mother. She had never bothered to wonder much about Marc, the man whom Jeanne had said was Sylvie's father. Now she did.

When she went home, she would ask Jeanne how she had met Marc, and how she had felt, and why she had decided not to marry him.

She thought that she could almost like Lyon as it was now in the quiet darkness by the river, with the city buildings all around them in the bright moonlight.

"I loved Lyon from the first time I saw it," Robert said abruptly. "You're looking at the Cathédrale Saint-Jean?"

"Yes."

"It's not beautiful. Oh, they tried, or thought

they did, but it took over three centuries to build, and fashions kept changing, so nothing looks like it belongs with anything else. Inside there's an astronomical clock." He grinned. His gravity dropped away entirely. "You should see it. Automatons pop out of the clock every hour in the afternoon and act out the Annunciation. One of them's a rooster. He's my favorite."

"Automatons?"

"Little mechanical figures. They're powered by the clock mechanism. Have you never seen one?"

"No," Sylvie said dubiously. Mechanical figures. It did not sound like her kind of thing.

They had reached the church. "I'll show you," said Robert. He guided Sylvie around to the side and pushed gently on a heavy wooden door. It swung ponderously open. "This way."

Inside, the cathedral was dimly lit by candles. Sylvie had never been in so large a church; her footsteps echoed on the stone floors and the roof rose high overhead. She saw a pile of rags at one end of a pew; only after they had passed did the image resolve itself in her mind into a beggar, curled up to sleep, for even in this rich city full of houses,

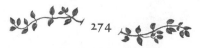

there were people without homes who came to the church for help. Up toward the front, a monk prayed on his knees, oblivious of his surroundings. Sylvie followed Robert, without speaking, to the left side of the huge cathedral.

"There," he whispered, pointing upward. The clock facade was ornate and gilded. She could see the little figures he'd mentioned: Mary and the angel Gabriel. The rooster.

She said, unbelieving: "They move?"

"Yes," said Robert with satisfaction. "They make an enormous racket. It could wake the dead." He laughed a little, low. "I love the noise."

Sylvie stared up at the clock. It was hard to see its details in the dimness, in the distance. "I would like to see it work," she said. It surprised her. "So would Martin. Could we—do you suppose we could come back tomorrow?"

She knew the answer from the fact that it took a moment or two for him to reply. "It wouldn't be wise," he said finally. "We should leave very early. But perhaps we could stop on our way back."

Sylvie nodded. "Fine."

Silence again. In it, Sylvie felt him turn back into

Robert. Finally she said what she had meant to say. "I have something to ask you. And something to tell you. May I?"

He said, "Yes."

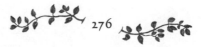

They sat together in a pew at the very back of the cathedral, far from the beggar and the monk, who still prayed at the altar; neither had stirred since Sylvie first noticed them. Sylvie thought of Monsieur Lehmann and of Madame du Bois's friend the archbishop. She wondered what the monk was praying for, and if his prayers would be answered. People always prayed that their prayers would be heard, but it was not the same thing as having them answered. Answers were often not what you expected.

Her prayer—her hope—to find a teacher had not been answered. Or perhaps it had, in an oblique way.

Sylvie turned slightly and looked directly at Robert, and at the shadows that the candlelight threw on his face. She said, "Robert, do you believe in God?"

He looked at her honestly. After a time, he said, "I like being in churches like this, at night, when few people are about. I can think well at such times."

She digested that. "Do you pray?"

"No." He turned to face her, his expression unreadable. Then he said bluntly, "I don't understand you. I thought you wanted to ask me about Ceciline. About why I—why I almost left you there, with her, even after I learned what she was. When I understood how she had betrayed me with her double game. Do you ask for my apology? I will give it to you freely."

Sylvie took in a deep breath. She had seen why it had been so difficult for Robert, from Madame du Bois's mind. But she did not know if she could tell him what she knew, or if she should. It was, in a way, yet another betrayal, to know such things about someone else when they had not told you themselves. She bit her lip. "Do I need to know why you hesitated? I know what you actually did in the end."

"Is that enough?" He sounded as if it would not be for him.

He sounded as if he wanted to tell her. She took a deep breath and said the truth, if not all of it. "I

 277

dislike to ask you to tell it, if it is bad. You are enti-
tled to privacy."

He said quietly: "It *is* bad. But you must ask me
to tell you, or I will not. It is *your* choice, to know
or to not know."

Sylvie focused her eyes on the row of yellow
flames that lit the path up the main aisle of the
cathedral to the altar.

He said, "You deserve to know."

He does want to talk, Sylvie thought. But he
cannot, he will not, unless I ask him. He needs to
be certain that I want to hear. She thought about
that first night with Ceciline, in Montigny. How it
had felt to finally speak of what she had done. How
it had been healing. Insight struck her: this was a
way *anyone* could heal—to talk, to listen. No special
powers were necessary. No special knowledge or
herbs or skills.

"Tell me," she said.

She knew most of it already, but it was different to hear him tell the story. He was quite dispas-
sionate about the boy he had been, the thief and
worse, while she bled inside for him and for what
he had had to do to survive. "Whatever her motives,

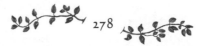

278

without her I would have starved," he said at the end about Ceciline. "I would never have learned to read and write. I would never have become who I am. I will always owe her.

"And she is more vulnerable than she herself knows. In Montigny, she is hated. I always wondered why she stayed once we had money." He laughed a little. "Ironic that all the while she had moved here to Lyon, and I didn't know. Yet I know she needs to be watched. And I'll watch her.

"But . . . I can't just take my business and leave her. She'd die, Sylvie. Everything that she said about your danger—it's just as true for her. I can protect her. And I will, for as long as she lives."

Sylvie was silent.

"Please understand," said Robert. She had never heard that word from him before. *Please.* How astonishing that he would plead for Ceciline and not himself.

"I'm listening," Sylvie said. It was all she could say past the obstruction in her throat.

"I wouldn't have left you with her, not for long. Believe that. I was just . . . trying to think of a way not to."

She managed to say, "I believe you," and it was true.

She thought he was finished. There was a long quiet time, and she had almost put herself back together, almost kept herself from crying. But then he added: "She's as close to a mother as I ever had, you see."

And then Sylvie could not help herself.

Robert said: "Sylvie? Sylvie, what is it? Come here."

His arms were warm and enveloping. She could feel his heart and hear the concern in his voice.

She cried.

When she could, Sylvie said: "I have a mother."

Robert stroked her hair. With one gentle finger, he wiped away her tears. He said: "Tell me about her."

"It is bad," said Sylvie, just as he had done. "Not—not about her. It's bad about me."

"I'm not afraid of your secrets," said Robert. "Any more than you seem afraid of mine. Tell me."

In the dim of the church, Sylvie did.

CHAPTER

Twenty-Six

They went to Marseille. The sun shone the whole way, and the air grew warm and gentle. As they traveled, Sylvie taught Martin to read.

And the days and weeks passed, and spring became summer, and then autumn was nearly upon them.

One night, on the barge as they returned to Lyon, Robert spoke privately to Sylvie. "Now that we have finished our business in Marseille, what is next? Home immediately?"

"Home immediately," she said.

He nodded; it was no surprise, for they had talked often. "I will take you and Martin." He paused. "You realize Martin will not stay long in Bresnois?"

"I know full well he belongs more to you than me now," Sylvie said dryly.

"Perhaps somewhat more." After a moment, Robert added: "You could, too. If you chose." His voice was calm and courteous, almost emotionless, but she knew him well now. "Or rather, I could belong to you. I find I like thinking of it that way." Now, emotion colored his voice, if only a little. "I—I very much wish for this, Sylvie. For us."

For all their talk, healing conversations that had ranged deeply into both of their pasts, this was the first time this topic had arisen again. Yet Sylvie had known it would come. She was prepared. She had thought long and hard, and she knew Robert would have done the same.

She reached out silently now and took his hand. Not to probe his mind; she would never do that. It was merely to feel his skin and the warmth when his hand enclosed hers.

For all their talk, in all these weeks, this was the first time they had touched.

He turned her to face him.

"What do you wish for, Sylvie?" he asked. "Tell me."

She looked up at him in the autumn moonlight. "Time," she said quietly. "Perhaps two or three years."

"Time with your mother."

"And time with myself. I have—discoveries to make."

"I know this." He nodded and added slowly, as if reluctantly, "I am not surprised. I must confess that I—I might need that time for myself, too. It's only—I don't want to lose you, Sylvie. It is a risk, parting. Seeing each other rarely."

"You want to seal the deal," Sylvie said, smiling. "It is your nature. But you know it is not mine."

He smiled then too. "Yes. I accept that. And if I cannot seal the deal, I will settle for hope." His face went solemn then. "May I have it?"

"Hope you may have," said Sylvie formally. "I have hope, too, for all that we are so different." She

looked searchingly up into his eyes, which were no longer cool and expressionless and never again would be, not for her. "You realize that you and I will but rarely be of the same mind? It would not be an *easy* marriage."

He laughed down at her.

"Well, it had to be said out loud!" Sylvie said.

"Did it? It is not exactly news to me," said Robert dryly. "But we have one thing in common. When times are difficult, we both can maneuver. We do not despair."

"Difficulty prompts one to seek solutions," said Sylvie demurely. "To look harder. To be creative." She moved a little closer to him. "To take risks."

"Yes," he said. "Exactly."

⁓

Some weeks later, Sylvie approached her mother's cottage. She came alone. She had insisted on it. There would be time for Robert to meet Jeanne later.

She had left Martin and Robert behind with Martin's family. They had only arrived that morning. She and Robert had followed Martin uncertainly

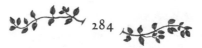

into the farrier's stable. A dull pounding told them that Martin's father was hard at work.

"Hello, Papa," Martin said in a pause between bangs.

The farrier's back stiffened. Slowly, his head turned, and he looked up from the horse he was shoeing. His eyes skimmed unbelievingly past Robert, who was dressed almost as well as if he were in the city, and then paused for a heart-beat on Sylvie. But then they focused entirely and completely on Martin.

His face reddened. He stood up. Without missing a beat, he began yelling at the top of his lungs while lunging leftward to grab his whip. "You stupid boy! I'll teach you a thing or two about running away!"

But before Sylvie or Robert could intervene, the farrier's yells stopped abruptly. His arm dropped. There was a short silence. Then he said quite calmly to Martin: "Idiot. Thought you'd scare us, did you? If we hadn't figured you were with Sylvie there . . ." Belatedly, he nodded at Sylvie. Once more, his gaze paused curiously on Robert. Then he scowled at

Martin again. "You were gone long enough. I never ran away for more than a week at your age."

Tentatively, Martin grinned. His father stiffened again. "I might whip you still, boy," he warned. "After dinner." He didn't embrace his son. He was not that kind of man. He stood there with his arms dangling by his sides, the red fading from his face. "Your brothers are out back," he said. "They'll beat you if I don't."

Sylvie winced, but Martin did not appear to mind. "Papa," he said. "Listen. I'm going to be apprenticed." He gestured at Robert. "This is Monsieur Chouinard. He's got a trading business. I'm already starting to learn"—Martin rolled the words out impressively—"Italian double-entry bookkeeping."

"Oh, really?" said the farrier. But his eyes examined Robert carefully, despite himself, a little awed. "What's that? Does it have to do with horses?"

"No," said Martin. "It's—"

Robert cut him off. "You and I will have to discuss apprenticeship terms, of course," he said formally to the farrier. "But I think Martin will be of use."

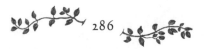

"Oh, he's bright," said the farrier. "Just laz—uh, not used to following orders."

"I can train him out of that," said Robert. His mouth twisted humorously. "Maybe."

"We'll be a good team," said Martin impertinently, and that earned him at long last the cuff from his father. But, Sylvie noticed, it wasn't very hard. And the farrier's hand lingered a few seconds longer on Martin's shoulder, gripping it hard.

"He will come home for visits at least once each year," said Robert.

"And bring the news of the world," Martin had said.

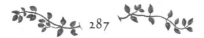

Now, standing outside her mother's cottage, Sylvie remembered that successful reunion and took a deep breath.

The door was open. Martin's father had said that Jeanne would be here. She had not been quite herself, he said, since Sylvie left. He had fumbled for words. "Vague," he said. "In her mind. Not about helping people, but . . ." He shrugged. "Other things." He'd given her a straight look. "Everyone will be glad you are back."

Fear tightened in Sylvie's stomach. She avoided the farrier's curious eyes. She could not even look at Martin or Robert, who fully understood what had happened with Jeanne.

"I'm home now," she had said to the farrier. "I will go to her."

⌒

She took one more deep breath and rapped loudly on the cottage's open door. "Hello?" she said. And then tentatively, "Jeanne?" For she dared not say *Maman*.

A figure formed out of the shadows within. "Yes? Hello? Does someone need me?"

Jeanne was as tall as ever, and as upright. She held a branch of juniper in her hand. Her smiling eyes met Sylvie's easily. "Hello, there." Then she frowned. "Do I know you?"

Sylvie could not speak.

Jeanne was shaking her head. "I feel sure I know you. And yet . . ."

"We've met before," Sylvie managed.

Jeanne's face cleared a bit. "I think I remember now. Wasn't it early last spring? You're a healer, too, aren't you? You spent a night here. Yes, that's

it. That must be it." She smiled, pleased with herself and clearly, too, a little relieved. "Come in." She laughed. "I haven't the world's best memory, I'm afraid."

Sylvie winced. She followed her mother into the cottage and sat, as directed, at the table while Jeanne bustled about with tea. When Jeanne asked, she said: "My name is Sylvie."

Jeanne laughed. "Wood sprite. What a perfect name for a healer!"

"Yes," said Sylvie. "I suppose." She listened to Jeanne chatter as she looked about with wonder. Everything was exactly the same as it had been. She felt carefully, guiltily, in her mind for the piece of her mother that she had carried with her over so many miles. It was there. She still did not know how to restore it.

Nonetheless, she had been gifted, and no matter what lay ahead, she would use her gift. Carefully now. She would learn as much as she could, from whomever she could.

Perhaps she was not meant to have one single teacher. She had learned from Ceciline, from Robert, from Martin, from Arnaud . . .

She would be careful of others, aware as she now was of the harm she might do. And she would be careful that she might live in this world that was increasingly hostile to women such as herself. This world that misunderstood and called them evil. There would be times when, for various reasons, she could not be fully herself.

But even in those times, she could heal. A true healer would never turn away just because she did not have a magical cure. Indeed, the best cures were not always magical. Had not Jeanne shown her that, all her life? And Robert. Robert had not needed magic to begin healing. Or, indeed, to help Sylvie heal.

Words that could be spoken, and ears that could listen, and—once, in a grand cathedral—arms that could hold, had been magic enough.

That, and time.

Sylvie could not magically restore the memories she had taken from Jeanne. Not now, and perhaps not ever. But she was still her mother's daughter. And if there was no magical cure, she would find another way. She would work as Jeanne did, in the

dark, feeling her way forward, with hope, and with prayer, and with faith.

She was a healer.

She drank Jeanne's tea. Jeanne fidgeted with her own. "I wonder," Jeanne said finally, "if you would stay a while, here in Bresnois, with me?" And when Sylvie did not reply immediately, she rushed on, flushing a little: "I could use some help. I know you will have your own life and plans, of course. But . . ." She faltered.

"Yes," said Sylvie. She cleared her throat and began again, firmly. "Yes. I can stay for a time. Perhaps—a year or two? I am young. I would like to learn from you."

Jeanne's whole face came alight. "Good," she said, and smiled the smile that Sylvie recognized, even if Jeanne did not. It said, *You are my daughter, and I love you.*

And you are my mother, thought Sylvie, and I love you. One day she would say it aloud.

In time. She would have faith.

Jeanne was saying eagerly: "It will be wonderful to have you here. Perhaps we can learn from

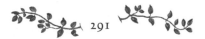

each other. Perhaps we'll become friends." She looked down then and added a little diffidently: "Here all alone . . . with no one to talk to about these things . . . I've been feeling lonely for another healer."

"Yes, I understand," said Sylvie quietly. "So have I." And she reached out and took her mother's hand.